UNSETTLED

ZACH JENKINS

Unsettled

Zach Jenkins

Copyright © 2017 Zach Jenkins

ISBN-13: 978-1546904083
ISBN-10: 1546904085

Want to be the first to know
about Zach Jenkins' latest release?
Want to receive his bonus stories not available anywhere else?
Sign up for his newsletter at:
http://zpjenkins.com/newsletter-unsettled/

UNSETTLED

Zach Jenkins

PROLOGUE

Carter

The door banged shut behind me, drowning out most of the noise of the club. All that I could hear in the dark alley was the thumping of the bass from the track the DJ was playing and my own breathing, coming in short, shallow gasps. This amazing night was about to go supernova.

"Right here, Trey?" I asked. "Are you sure? My apartment is only a few blocks away and my roommates won't be home until the club closes. We'll have hours before they get there."

Trey smiled.

I swooned, willing to do whatever he asked. The man must have been an angel sent down to Earth to give lonely guys like me one perfect night. Out of all the men in the club who had hoped to catch Trey's attention, I was the one who'd won...at least for one night.

I knew it wouldn't last any longer than that. Trey bounced like a hummingbird from flower to flower, taking whatever he wanted, and not a single person that he'd fucked had ever complained.

And now it was my turn.

Trey towered over me. His dick, still trapped inside his pants, but hard and huge, pressed against my stomach.

My mouth watered. I needed him now, but I still hoped he'd accept my offer to go back to my apartment so I could explore his body more fully than I'd ever manage in the alley. If I was only going to get one chance, I wanted to make the most of it.

"Baby doll," Trey purred. "We're not going to need all that time. Time's so arbitrary anyway. There's pleasure to be found in all kinds of things. Like my 'fro. That didn't happen overnight, and each day it brings me new pleasure. Someday, I'll get tired of it, and I'll drag the clippers from the back of my closet and buzz it all down. Wham bam. And I'll enjoy that, too. Carter, man, you're a wham-bam pleasure. I just want to bust my nut all over you."

Somewhere in the back of my head, I knew what he said wasn't exactly flattering, but lust and my strong beer buzz over-ruled that thought. All I heard was my name.

Trey knows my name!

I would have done whatever he'd asked.

He didn't ask me to do anything, though. He just stood there with a smile on his face while he looked out in the distance, as if talking to someone else in an entirely different dimension.

But I still knew what I was supposed to do.

I dropped to my knees, unzipped his pants, and took his dick in my hand. Trey's dick. As long and beautiful as I'd imagined whenever I'd watched him dancing over the last few months. Smooth as glass, and twice as hard, I wrapped both of my hands around it and wondered how any other dick would ever be able to bring me pleasure.

"That's right. Stroke it and suck it for me," Trey said, his hands calmly on his hips as if things like this were an everyday occurrence.

The cocky bastard. I wished I had the strength to stand up and walk away, but we both knew I didn't have it in me.

In my lamest act of defiance ever, I spat on that dick instead of sucking it. *Take that.* But then I caved and started rubbing my spit up and down his thick cock as I leaned forward to lick the tip.

"That's right, you dirty fuck. Suck my dick."

And I did.

Cars drove past the mouth of the alley. Dogs from who the fuck knew where barked. And I stayed on my knees enthusiastically sucking Trey's dick until long after my knees screamed in pain and my jaw felt like it had split in two. It might have been days or years. Time really was arbitrary with Trey.

He finally grabbed the back of my head and fucked my face with a force that took my breath away. No one would believe Trey's wildness when I told them the story. Well, they might, but they wouldn't realize just how crazy it had been. When he finally exploded in my mouth, he held me firmly in place until I'd swallowed the load to avoid it dribbling out and staining my shirt.

I didn't struggle. I wanted the moment to last as long as possible. It was just like that with Trey.

Only when he was certain that I'd swallowed, did he finally release me.

"Damn. Not half bad, Carter."

I blushed, half from shame at the thought that I could have been better. But how could anyone be good enough for Trey?

As he pulled his dick back into his tight pants, and tugged up on the zipper, I managed to find the nerve to ask, "Is it my turn now, Trey?"

He shook his head. "Not quite, little man. I need you to do me a favor and it needs done quick, if you know what I mean. Take this down to the alley by the bank," he pointed to the west while handing me a thick envelope he pulled from his back pocket. "Give it to my friend and hurry back and I'll give you what you need."

Almost every fiber in my body screamed, "No!"

I'd heard all the rumors that Trey was troubled, maybe even

mixed up in drug dealing or worse. But with my dick strained against my jeans, whatever it took to end up in Trey's mouth seemed like a small price to pay.

Fuck.

I looked around the alley, knowing I wouldn't see any kind of sign telling me what to do, but needing to buy some time.

Trey just stood there, holding the envelope out for me, looking like he had no doubt what I'd decide.

He was right. I cursed my weakness as I pulled the package from his grip.

"There you go," Trey said. "Hop off like a good bunny and then hurry back and Trey will take good care of your needs."

I was running before I got to the end of the alley, desperate to see my dick between Trey's lips.

Once I turned onto the main street, though, I slowed. Attracting attention would only have delayed my return. I flinched at every noise during the short walk, promising to never end up in a similar situation again.

I mean, I knew I was committing a crime, but one time couldn't hurt. I'd drop the package off, hurry back to Trey, and get my dick sucked in reward. Afterward, I'd never come anywhere near The Strip again. I'd stay over on my side of Augusta, Georgia. I'd lock myself in the library on campus, study my ass off until I finished my degree. Then I'd move to California and never come back.

"Stop right there!" someone shouted from the shadows further down another alley. I hadn't made it to the bank yet. Had Trey given me the wrong directions?

I froze and raised my hands above my head.

"What's the password motherfucker?"

What did Trey get me involved with?

"Password? I don't know. Trey just said—"

"Shut up! Tell me the fucking password!"

"I don't know. Trey said to give you the package. That's all."

The man, still hidden in the shadows, laughed.

I felt entirely exposed and vulnerable, but didn't even consider running. Surely a man that did drug deals in alleys would be armed.

Get this done and just go home. Fuck, Trey.

I was just about to set the envelope on the ground and hope the stranger would let me back away when a voice from the street behind me shouted, "Halt!"

Trapped.

"Who are you working for?" the new voice asked.

I answered immediately and with no concern about protecting anyone. "Trey. He said to meet these guys, hand them the envelope, and that's it. I don't even know what's in it."

"You should have stayed away from Trey, kid. He's sent you to the wrong part of town."

I heard the shot at the same time that the bullet tore a hole in my back. I dropped the envelope as I fell to my knees. The thought that I was spending entirely too much time on my knees flashed through my mind before another shot tore into my back.

I rolled onto my back, hoping to at least see the stars one more time before the sick fuck killed me. The clouds denied me that chance, but did give me the chance to see my attacker.

He wore a blue shirt, a black hat. When he took a step toward me, the light flashed against the badge on his chest.

A cop? That doesn't make any sense.

Before I could solve the mystery, he fired one last shot.

1

JAMES

*T*rey Anderson moved with a grace that shouldn't have been possible in a six-and-a-half-foot-tall man, especially one wearing pink combat boots that elevated him another three inches. Towering over the crowd, his hips swayed and bounced from man to man without settling on anyone, just like Trey himself.

I'd forced myself to come to The Firehouse, the only gay dance club on the block of Augusta that we called The Strip, for the fifth night in a row because once and for all, I was going to make my move on Trey. One way or the other, he'd know exactly how I felt after months of watching him from afar, trying to decide if I was man enough to actually do something about the desire he'd awoken in me ever since the night I'd arrested him for wandering the streets, drunk and loud after the bars had shut down.

I considered heading home early. There'd been a brutal murder in the city the previous night. One of the college kids seemed to have gotten himself mixed up in some kind of drug deal that had gone sour. It had only been a few blocks away from The Firehouse. We hoped that we weren't at the beginning of one of the crime sprees that always seemed to pop up during the hottest parts of summer. Until we found a solid lead, though, we were just grasping in the dark.

Each time I tried to stand and either leave or make my way across the dance floor to profess my—*what? Certainly not love. Maybe lust. Undying infatuation? Extreme curiosity?*—I chickened out. His eyes always seemed to pick that moment to lock onto mine for a split second that lasted an eternity. His long, thick, gold-colored lashes had to be fake. As was the rainbow glitter that covered his face and sparkled like stars. Still, as his undulations made the light reflect at different angles, I longed to wake up next to Trey and see what he looked like on a normal morning while we made breakfast together and he talked about what a great lay I was.

Just when I would remember that breathing was a thing, I'd realize he wasn't looking at me at all anymore and I'd have to start the whole process of screwing up my courage all over again.

My fingers begged to rub across his smooth, dark skin. My lips screamed to be kissed by his bright red lips. My flesh was oh-so-willing, but my spirit was a fucking coward.

Raising my hand to flag down the shot boy for another one of those glowing green vodka shots, I leaned back in my chair, giving in to another night of futility, and cursing the difficulty of being a male cop in Georgia who wanted to fuck another man.

Moving wasn't an option. My family needed me as much as I needed them. They dragged me out of the house and made me talk to humans instead of drinking my way to oblivion. I was my sister's frequent babysitter. It felt like an even trade on most days.

The shot boy, wearing a white halter top and a very short, very pink skirt, wove through the crowd and sat down on my lap before I had a chance to protest. His tiny ass landed squarely on my dick, forcing me to grunt as I shifted to get more comfortable.

Watching Trey had left me hard and horny.

Sean's eyes went wide. "Officer James. I never dreamed you'd be so happy to see me."

I didn't bother telling him to use my last name. If he hadn't started after the first few reminders, another wasn't going to help.

When he shifted his hips, my eyes closed. If I wasn't careful, I was going to end up taking the shot boy home. "Get off me, Sean. We've been over this before. You're not my type."

"Too fem?" he asked, while he rubbed the back of my neck with his free hand.

"No," I said without further detail. Blunt worked best with Sean. Give him an inch...well, he'd want more than just the tip.

My attention was once again sucked in by Trey's gravitational pull. Three men pressed against his long, lean body. Based on their haircuts, they were from the Army base on the other side of town. The college kids were the same age, but normally had longer, floppier hair. The soldiers looked determined to each have a turn with Trey, and for more than just dancing. Before I could use that as my excuse to rush to his side, Trey effortlessly spun away from them all. Before they even noticed he was gone, Trey had made his way to the DJ booth that really wasn't anything more than a raised platform with a rickety wooden railing around the perimeter and a table with his equipment facing the crowd.

"Oh," Sean said. "You like something a little darker?"

"What?" I gasped. "No. I mean, he's gorgeous, but it's not that. It's his presence," I said before realizing I was still talking out loud.

Sean patted my cheek. "Yeah, baby, we all feel that about Trey. But Trey is ephemeral on the best of days. He's barely real when he *does* notice anyone. You can do better for yourself than Trey. Not me, of course. I'm too...whatever, I suppose. But Trey will just break your heart and not even notice that he did it." Sean held a shot to my lips and poured it into my mouth. "On the house, Officer James. Just don't torment yourself with guys like Trey who are just looking for a quick fuck. A solid, real man like you needs a solid, real man to appreciate just how solid you can be." He wiggled his butt against my dick again, making me groan.

I forced my credit card into Sean's hand. Despite never having seen him outside the club, Sean was as close to a friend as I had, which said everything that needed to be said about my social life. "Add five bucks for your tip, Sean."

Sean's sigh was full of disappointment at my rejection of the free drink, but he took the card and skipped away to take the orders from a group of men in suits before heading back to handle my bill.

Hoping that the men in suits would be able to tip Sean better than I could on my cop salary, I turned my attention back to the DJ booth and was surprised to see Trey and the DJ both looking right at me. I knew the DJ, kind of. He was my neighbor. He'd moved in sometime in March and other than grunting at each other while getting the mail or taking out the trash, we'd never talked to each other.

Both men laughed when they saw that I'd noticed their attention. The DJ quickly turned back to the turntable and did something that added the chorus of a song on top of the techno beat that the crowd was dancing to. Somehow it worked.

Trey smiled, blew me a kiss, and waved me over.

Holy shit.

With Trey's full attention on me, my face became hot. I wanted to run away. I certainly couldn't trust my unsteady legs to carry me across the room, but somehow they did without me even telling them to. I was a puppet to Trey's whims. Warning bells went off in my head.

This is a bad idea.

Sean's warning niggled at the back of my mind, but how could I say no when Trey beckoned?

"Hey," I said lamely while leaning against the DJ booth, and trying to look calm and collected.

"You're a cop, right?" Trey asked.

As his lips moved, all I could see was the speck of glitter on the lower left side of his lip. I wanted to nibble it off. Trey's lip curled up on that side in a cruel smile that implied he knew exactly what I wanted.

"Yeah, I know you," he continued. "You busted my ass one time. Took me into the station. But they let me go because they know that there's no earthly walls that can contain Trey Anderson."

Finding a tiny bit of my spine, I answered, "After you paid the fine. I'm sure that helped a little bit."

"Sure, baby. But that's part of the magic of Trey. I always have the Benjamins for when a smile or a little poke from my magic stick won't do the trick."

He laughed when my eyes dropped toward his crotch at the mention of his dick.

Certain that Trey was teasing and had no interest in me, I was stunned when he asked, "So what's your scene, man? You down to clown around?"

Images of the carnal acts I wanted to perform with Trey flashed through my head. He certainly wouldn't be interested in a long-term relationship. I wasn't either, though. I didn't think so, at least. But for a quick fuck to decide if I really wanted to be with men or just needed to try once, Trey could be just what I needed.

Still, something felt off. Like I was being baited into a trap. A quick nod felt safer than agreeing too loudly. I tried to claim it was cop instinct, but knew it was more likely just my cowardice storming back.

"Hot damn, officer man. We thought you'd never get up the nerve."

"We?" It came out as much more of a squeak than I'd intended.

Fuck no. I'm not about to get gang banged by Trey and his friends.

"Yeah, we. But close your mouth, horn dog. I was curious

when you'd man up, but I'm not joining you and Evan. Evan deserves your proper attention. And don't let me hear that you didn't give him your utmost, undivided attention or you'll have me to answer to, got it?"

The room spun and went silent as the song ended abruptly and none followed after it. I felt every eye in the club on me as I tried to make sense of what Trey was saying.

He doesn't want to fuck me.

Fine.

But he wants me to fuck someone else?

Who?

The crowd started to boo as I hesitated with my answer.

When the music started again and the crowd cheered, I realized *they* weren't waiting for my answer. They were waiting for the DJ who had dropped the ball and left them without the beat they needed to feed their frenzy.

The DJ. My neighbor. He must be Evan.

He couldn't have been over five and a half feet tall. More than six inches shorter than me. He practically disappeared in his giant hoodie, just like he had most of the times I'd seen him taking out the trash. His head shook a firm rejection of Trey's meddling. He then flashed both middle fingers at Trey, who laughed as he shimmied back to the dance floor, blowing us each a kiss as the masses swarmed around him in an adoring cocoon.

I turned back to my neighbor—Evan, according to Trey—but he'd already turned his attention back to poking his laptop with one hand and a turntable with the other, clearly forgetting about me as quickly as Trey had.

"Sorry about that," I mumbled, feeling that something needed to be said, but Evan made no indication that he'd heard.

I needed to get the fuck out of the swarm of chaotic thoughts that were attacking me. Trey had rejected me, and had even tried to pass me off to another man. And *that man* had rejected me, too. If that wasn't a sign to stay away from men, despite how hard my cock got when I looked at some of them, I didn't know what it would take.

Pushing my way through the crowd, I ignored Sean, who was calling my name. I needed fresh air. Unfortunately, the air outside the bar was nearly as hot and stale as inside. After living all thirty years of my life in Georgia, I still found the summer heat unbearable some nights. Not for the first time, I thought about getting away. My sister could find another babysitter. I could send her money if she needed it. Or maybe she could finally force the baby's dad to pay for his kid.

Fucking Rick.

Problem for another day.

I needed beer from cans, and country music. Dance clubs were never going to be my scene and, since Trey had firmly shot me down, I couldn't think of a single reason to ever go back to one of them.

2

EVAN

*B*efore I turned off the piece-of-shit Porsche 911 I'd gotten for a steal right before moving away from home several years back, the check engine light came on again. The car was older than I was and the clicking noise it made when idling was just one more opportunity for me to pump money that I didn't have into the dying beast. I'd have to take it over to Will and see if he could work on it after hours again and save me a few dollars.

My house's detached garage opened to an alley that I was usually uncomfortable walking through to get home. Other than the one behind The Firehouse that I frequented for smoke breaks, alleys creeped me out. Short, gay, and quick-tempered was not the best combination for staying out of trouble, especially so close to The Strip. With all the bars and strip clubs, bad things seemed to congregate in that area.

Much like the car, though, I was too poor to do much about it.

Looks like it's time to start walking to and from work for a while. It's not like I go anywhere else, so what's the point in fixing the car?

The garbage can on the side of the garage got a swift kick

when it reminded me that it was completely my fault that I didn't make more money. Gay and quick-tempered was actually safe enough for the alley most days, but it never worked for me in the corporate world. After getting fired from six office jobs in two years, I gave up a few years back and learned to rely on the money I made DJing at The Firehouse. It paid just well enough to keep me fed and stocked in cigarettes. As long as ramen noodles, frozen pizza, and macaroni and cheese counted as real food.

Needing a smoke to calm my nerves, I grabbed the one that I'd tucked behind my ear and reached into my pocket for my lighter, but only found my keys and a condom that one of the waitresses gave me as a gag earlier in the night.

Extra small.

Word had gotten out after I'd made the mistake of fucking one of the bartenders. I was most definitely not an extra-small in that department. Three waitresses had given me their numbers in the last week, hoping that I liked pussy, too.

Sorry, ladies.

Fortunately, that bartender got canned for stealing some money. He seemed like a clinger and I was definitely not in the right mental place for a relationship.

The condom reminded me that I wouldn't be needing even an appropriately sized one.

Fuck you, Trey. Why'd he have to scare off my cop?

I threw the condom across the yard, and gave the cigarette an evil look. I should have quit smoking, too. Stupid expensive habit, but fuck that. I'd already quit drinking. No smoking? What'd be next? No fucking? No breathing?

Breathe. Relax. Five. Four. Three. Two. One. Breathe out.

I'd seen a therapist six times back in high school when my parents were trying to turn me straight. The only thing I'd gotten out of it was that soothing technique before I'd started skipping appointments and eventually just moved away from home after

high school graduation to save everyone the grief and embarrassment of being around me.

Standing in the hot early morning in my own backyard, an
hour from my family, everything was good enough, though, except
for my busted car and that god-awful country music the cop was
listening to out on his back porch. It was bad enough that he'd
shunned me earlier. He didn't need to rub it in by playing that
shitty honky-tonk music at three o'clock in the morning. There
was no way I'd fall asleep until he went to bed and turned it off.

Without pausing to consider the consequences, I stomped
through his yard. Just as I reached the first step of the back porch,
I considered that this cowboy-loving cop might be sitting there
drinking away memories of a dog that had just died, and hugging
up to his shotgun.

*Don't be stupid. Not everyone that listens to country music in
Georgia is a cowboy with a shotgun fetish.*

"Howdy, partner," a deep voice drawls from a dark corner of
the covered porch.

*Shit. I should have just gone to bed and turned on my radio loud
enough to drown out his. I've got to learn to control my impulses.*

The porch creaked as he rose from his porch swing. All I
could see was his shadow, which reminded me that he was damn
tall, but at least there was no sign of a shotgun.

Desperate to go on the offensive and keep any advantage I
might have had, I said, "Turn down that shitty music, man," and
cringed at how loud my voice sounded. I couldn't back down,
though. "It's too late for that shit. It's after 1965 after all."

"What are you? Some kind of music vigilante doing a sweep
of the city to keep the citizens safe from music you don't like?
After listening to that stuff you call music down at The Firehouse,
I needed to scrub it from my ears. Besides, it's not that loud. No
one else is complaining. Why don't you just go to bed before you
say something you'll regret?"

"Don't you threaten me, man." I hoped I sounded bold and confident, but when my palms started sweating, I really wished I'd been able to smoke that cigarette. I didn't even know the guy's name. He was just some eye candy that I'd noticed in the club but couldn't work up the nerve to talk to. For all I knew, he was crazy.

When he stepped toward me, I felt so small. Him being a couple of steps above me wasn't helping anything. His body seemed to stretch up to the moon. My legs wobbled and time slowed. I felt drunk. Grabbing ahold of the handrail to steady myself, I took a good look at his face. At the club, I'd limited myself to side glances to make sure he didn't catch me gawking. I had trouble getting past the evening stubble that covered his strong jawline that I would have loved to have scratch up the insides of my legs.

When I noticed the cowboy hat, I lowered my eyes to stop myself from giggling, but it did nothing to help me regain my composure. His faded blue jeans were so tight I had no trouble telling that this cowboy would have no need for an extra-small condom, either.

Giddy-up!

I deserved a handsome, rugged, sturdy man, but this one had already turned me down once. I wouldn't be giving him another chance to hurt me.

He didn't say anything. Instead, he just stood there, as big and mysterious as the night, with an amused twinkle in his eyes and his mouth curving up into a grin.

"Just turn it off, okay?" I whispered, not sure if I was talking about the radio or whatever he was doing to make me hornier the longer he stared at me. I poked him in the chest with my fingertip to drive the point home. It was like touching granite. I immediately regretted another one of my foolish impulsive moves and hoped that the mountain of a man would not get mad at the provocation and decide to crush me.

Hoping to sidetrack the cop, I said, "I worked a long shift and got shit on at work by an asshole customer," I flash him a grin of my own. *Two can play at that game.* "I just want to climb into bed and fall asleep."

That was a lie. I was buzzing with energy, more alive than I'd been in years. Between needing a drink, a smoke, and a fuck, I knew I wouldn't sleep until I got at least one of them. I thrust my hands into my pockets again, searching for my lighter before remembering again that I'd left it at the bar. Growling in frustration, I tossed the cigarette out into the yard.

I'm not gonna drink. I'm not gonna fuck. I'll just light the damn cigarette on the stove.

But I couldn't do that, either. I'd just thrown out my last cigarette. I needed to go out in the morning to buy more.

When I turned back to look at the cop again, that wide, easy smile taunted my sensibilities. Could he possibly be interested? Grabbing the can of cheap, piss-flavored beer from the man's hand, I had it halfway to my lips before remembering.

No alcohol. I'm not going to end a three-year streak just because of this asshole.

I tossed the can over my shoulder where it joined my cigarette, lost to the night in the backyard.

"Hey, what the fuck?" he said, finally showing some sign that I was getting to him.

"Drink a real beer next time," I said, grimacing at how much of an asshole it made me sound. I should have just gone to bed. I closed my eyes and counted down again.

"You can't just come over here and steal my beer, you know?" the man said, a little too slowly for me to deal with.

I needed to burn off energy. I needed to bounce or spin or run.

Or fuck.

"Call the cops, man," I said. "It's just half of one cheap-ass can of beer. Lock me up." I held my wrists out as if waiting to be handcuffed, and wondered why I wasn't trying to be nicer to the man with the broad chest and tiny waist.

"I'm off duty," he said, hooking his thumbs in his belt loops and stepping down one stair. His legs moved with a hint of bowed legs that did nothing to help me feel steadier.

I couldn't tell if he intended to punch me or kiss me. Had I misread what had happened in the club? I certainly hadn't been his target when he'd come over to the DJ booth, but was it possible that he hadn't rejected me, but rather had been flustered by what Trey had said?

I wasn't good about backing down when confronted, even when it was clearly in my best interest, but I wasn't much good at fighting either. I was too small and pretty for that.

He didn't seem threatening, other than just being huge and awake at hours when civilized people should be sleeping. If I didn't know better, I'd have guessed that he thought the whole incident was amusing. Something he'd be able to joke about with his friends when he went back to work.

We stared at each other for long enough for my racing heart to pound several times.

What is he doing to me?

Before I could stop the words from pouring out of my mouth, I asked, "Do you want to fight or fuck? Because if neither, I'm going home."

I immediately wished I were anywhere else in the universe.

Stupid impulses.

I doubted that the cop would punch me, but I'd have to deal with him chuckling about what I'd just said every time we saw each other while walking to our garages or getting our mail.

The man turned back to the house without a word.

I exhaled, hoping the guy was too drunk to remember our meeting in the morning.

Just before I turned toward my own place, he opened his

screen door and said, "Are you gonna stand there or are you coming in?"

With no hesitation, I hurried up the steps. My cock sprang to attention when he pressed his hand against the small of my back and guided me through the door.

3

JAMES

What the hell did I get myself into?

Even with a bit of a beer buzz, I couldn't believe my audacity. A couple of hours earlier I'd run away from Evan at the club, but somehow he was inside my house, presumably planning to fuck me just a couple of hours later. I knew inviting him in had to be a horrible idea, one that I would regret in the morning. But since becoming a cop after college, I hadn't had nearly enough wild nights.

What could be wilder than fucking a man for the first time?

Even if he wasn't Trey.

I forced myself to slow down and take in the moment. So what if he wasn't Trey? Truth be told, I knew Trey was an unattainable asshole and I'd probably used that as an excuse to drive my desire for him. What could be safer than a man who would never be interested in me?

Evan was different. He *was* attainable. He'd asked me. He wanted me. At least for the night.

After locking my back door, I joined Evan in the living room. He'd already tossed his hoodie onto the couch. His black T-shirt was tight enough for me to get a good look at his chest, and I liked what I saw. Thin and compact.

When I'd imagined myself with a man, it was always someone freakishly fabulous like Trey. Watching Evan bouncing around, inspecting everything in my living room, made me realize that there were all kinds of fish in the sea. With his high cheekbones and serious, soulful eyes I looked forward to watching this one nibble on my line.

He swiped at his long, brown hair to tuck it behind his ears. "Nice place," he said, leaning forward to stare at a picture hanging on the wall. "Who's this?"

"My sister. It's us fishing during a camping trip. That's from right before she went away for college." She'd tried using college as a way out, but ended up back home after sophomore year, started dating Rick, and ended up pregnant with his baby. If the kid wasn't so cool, I would have thought she'd have been better off staying in college.

"You had hair," Evan said.

I rubbed my head and felt the rough stubble. "Yeah. Up until I joined the force. I'd be afraid of bald spots if I tried to grow it out now."

Everything was going wrong. Instead of rushing to my bed for sex, we were actually talking.

What if he figures out that I'm not interesting enough to be with?

As if reading my mind, he asked, "Got any condoms?"

I wasn't sure. Nearly in a panic, I pulled my wallet from my back pocket, hoping to find one inside. A wave of relief washed over me when I found one between two bills.

Proud of my trophy, I held it up for Evan to see.

"Just one?" he asked.

Oh, right. He'll want one too if he wants to fuck me. I swallowed while considering the implications, trying to decide if I was ready to let him penetrate me.

While I was distracted, he grabbed the condom from my

hand and checked the date. "Fine. Looks like we've just got one, though. Rock, paper, scissors for it?"

Evan laughed when I held out my hand, uncertainly.

"I'm kidding, man." He tossed the condom back to me. "Besides, there's nothing better than a nice dick rubbing against my prostate after a long night working. Those orgasms are so intense, right?"

My mouth failed to find words. He was doing such a good sales job for receiving, that I considered handing him the condom. How could I answer, though, having never tried it before?

"Upstairs or right here on the couch?" Evan asked with his hands tucked into his back pockets and his eyes locked onto my chest rather than reaching my face. "Your house. Your rules," he said while looking at me defiantly and making me feel like he suspected that I would back out.

Damn it, James? What do *you want?*

Evan cocked his head when I didn't answer right away. He looked like he'd just figured out that it was going to be my first time and was trying to decide how we'd gotten to the point of staring at each other across my living room. Or maybe I was projecting.

He's going to make the decision for me and leave if I don't get my ass in gear. What do I want?

"Upstairs," I managed to say.

Evan smiled and nodded. "Good. But before we go up there, I think I should make sure we're clear on something. I'm not looking for anything beyond tonight. Relationships just aren't my thing. We can fuck, and then we can still say hi when we bump into each other. If you're wanting more than that, we should just call it off right now. But if you're down for a fast, hard fuck tonight, let's have a little fun."

His words unleashed something in me. A night of meaningless sex with no attachments was exactly what I needed. Keep it simple.

"I thought I told you to get upstairs," I shouted, playfully swatting at his ass as he bounded toward the stairs with a giggle.

When we got to the bedroom, I groaned. "I don't have any lube."

"No lube?" Evan laughed. "What kind of gay guy doesn't have lube?" When I didn't reply, his eyes went wide at the realization. "What's going on here?"

"Does it matter?" I snapped. "One night. Hard, fast fuck, right? No attachments."

Evan nodded. "True." He pulled something from his pocket and tossed it at me. "Use this."

The thing in my hand looked like a packet of ketchup. "Lube in a packet? That's a thing?"

"Jesus Christ, man. Don't kill my boner."

Evan tugged the shirt over his head. His smooth, hairless chest was covered with brightly colored tattoos. With the shirt on, I would have never guessed he was inked since none spilled out past the end of his short sleeves.

I wanted to spend time exploring them, comparing them to my own, and asking why he'd never had any done on his arms, but Evan wasn't wasting any time. He unbuckled his belt and tossed it to the floor. He sat on the edge of my bed and wrestled out of his jeans. Then he was back on his feet before I'd managed to move.

The bounce of his hard cock reminded me exactly what was at stake.

I had no thoughts of backing down anymore, though. I tossed my shirt across the room. My dick pressed painfully against my pants. I pulled them off to give my dick room to breathe.

"Nice tats," Evan said.

I grunted in appreciation while tearing open the condom. With well-practiced ease, just never with a man watching, I rolled the condom on. I tore into the lube next, squeezed it on, and spread it with a firm rub that made me groan in need.

"Damn. You're not fucking around are you?" Evan asked. "Rock on. Let's do this." Evan lay down on his back and with his legs closed, pulled his knees close to his chest. "Get inside me, cowboy."

I was fighting against two very different needs.

On one hand, I wanted to take things slowly, and explore our bodies, and make a real experience of my first time with a man.

On the other hand, his asshole was begging to be fucked.

It felt rude not to comply.

Using my hand as a guide, I pressed against his entrance. The lube did its magic, and it only took a few seconds until I was inside Evan, staring in amazement as I started to make love...no, to fuck his ass.

There was no love, just lust.

Evan matched me grunt for grunt as we picked up the pace.

He grabbed his dick and started masturbating while I continued slamming against his body. Any thoughts I had of trying to take things slowly evaporated when I watched Evan's hand flying up and down his dick. He hadn't been joking around either when he'd said he wanted it hard and fast.

Pulling his legs against my chest, I wrapped my arms around his thighs and tried to fuck him so hard he'd forget to use his own hand. It didn't work, but based on the grunts and moans, I was doing exactly what he wanted.

Each time I tried to make eye contact, he'd turn his head to the side, giving me the reminder that there was no romance between us. Just two men fucking the demons out of their system.

I wondered briefly what his demons were before my balls tightened, giving me a split second's notice before I exploded. The orgasm shook through my body and forced a wild scream from my lips. I vaguely heard him grunting and groaning as he shot his own load that landed high up on his chest.

After an eternity where it felt like I would never stop coming, I fell onto the bed beside Evan, exhaustion threatening to overcome me before I saw him out the door.

Evan didn't move, but I was too tired to wonder why, after his earlier bravado about fucking and leaving, he was still there. He looked so peaceful lying next to me. I certainly had no intention of kicking him out of my bed.

Besides, I was wrestling with my own emotions. I'd just fucked a man and wasn't sure exactly what that meant.

Am I gay now? What about women? I'm still attracted to them. I must be at least a little gay, though.

I pushed aside that line of thinking after acknowledging that I would definitely be interested in sex with a man again in the future. Any further contemplation was silly at that point. It wasn't like I had any other men lined up. Trey had shot me down, and Evan had made it clear he wasn't looking for anything beyond the one time.

I knew I'd lied to myself earlier. I wasn't looking for meaningless sex, and I definitely wanted an attachment. And Evan's even breathing next to me was the perfect way to calm my soul and help me drift off to sleep.

It was too bad he didn't want more than just one night.

4

JAMES

*W*hen the doorbell woke me the next morning, I stretched lazily and smiled. The night's sleep had left me perfectly refreshed. What a crazy night. It had definitely been too long since I'd gotten laid.

"James, answer the door!" a woman screamed from the back porch: my sister.

I stretched again when my feet hit the floor. My mouth was dry. I always forgot to have a glass of water before falling asleep after drinking.

A groan from behind me on the bed sent me jumping to my feet. I turned and saw Evan, naked, hard, and sprawled out on the bed. I stared at the glorious sight until my sister rang the doorbell several more times in a row.

Shit.

After sliding into the jeans I'd been wearing the night before, and doing a quick, futile search for a shirt that didn't smell, I hurried down the stairs and opened the door.

"Good morning, Jillian."

She set Jeffrey on the floor where he quickly scurried to the living room, looking for the box of toys I kept for him under the coffee table.

"Oh my God, Jimmy," she started too loudly and dropped to a near whisper. I hated when she called me Jimmy. It made me feel like I was twelve. "That asshole."

She opened the fridge as if she'd said enough.

Making what felt like a safe guess, I asked, "What did Rick do this time?"

Rick being Jeffrey's father was bad enough. Unfortunately, he was also a fellow cop, and general prick. The combination of the three frequently made my life a living hell.

She slammed the orange juice bottle onto the counter and snapped at me. "That fucker cancelled."

I held a finger to my lip, pointed to her son in the living room, and tried not to laugh when Jillian shook her fists at the sky. "Sis, pretend I don't know what you're talking about and tell me what actually happened."

"He was supposed to watch Jeffrey for me this weekend—"

I knew how this story ended. "But something came up at work. He has to go out of town."

She pushed me squarely in the chest. "How do you know that?"

"Dude, we work together. I was in the meeting where he volunteered to represent us at the meeting in the capital when our normal rep for those things had to cancel. Better him than me."

There I went, putting myself squarely in the middle of another one of their constant fights again.

"What the fuck? He said the chief made him go," she said as if accusing me of being involved in Rick's shenanigans. I shook my head and shrugged. I regretted opening my stupid mouth. "So he deliberately lied to me, and now..."

Jillian trailed off when Evan shuffled into the kitchen in just his underwear. His pants, shirt and hoodie were tucked under his arm. At least his erection had gone away, but the tight boxer briefs left nothing to the imagination. I blushed at the memories from the night before. In the light of day, everything seemed raunchier. Rather than making me want to give up on him, though, I decided that I needed to find a way to get Evan back into my bed again despite his big talk of not wanting a relationship.

I was always up for a challenge.

Without a word, Evan set his clothes on the counter and poured some orange juice into a glass. He drank the entire thing before looking at us and saying, "Hey."

I would have laughed at how obvious it was that Evan was *not* a morning person if I hadn't felt my sister squeeze my elbow, silently demanding an explanation.

Evan rubbed his eyes and yawned. He managed to make even that look sexy.

"Yes, sorry, that's Evan. Evan, this is my sister, Jillian."

"Good morning, Evan," Jillian said giving his body another quick up-and-down before turning to raise her eyebrows at me. "You seem to have forgotten to wear your pants over to my brother's house."

Evan looked down at his mostly naked body. I took the chance to do the same.

He had to clear his throat before any words would come out. "Yeah, they're dirty and I just have to walk next door so..." he shrugged to indicate that was all there was to say about his state of dress.

"Of course," my sister said, indicating that she didn't agree one bit.

They all needed to get out of my house before things got any more awkward.

Evan nodded at me and Jillian. "All right. I should get going. Thanks for last night, James."

I took a step toward him before realizing that he had no intention of kissing me goodbye.

How did I manage to fuck a guy but never get around to kissing him?

If I did manage to talk Evan into another date—well, technically a first date, I supposed—I would make sure to correct that oversight.

As soon as Evan closed the door behind himself, Jillian cleared her throat.

"So, he seems nice." With the rising pitch at the end of the sentence, she left a million questions unasked.

"Yep. Good guy."

"Certainly not shy about, well, not wearing clothes." She wasn't going to let this go.

Deciding not to make it any easier for her, I answered, "Nope."

Trained by a lifetime of hiding potentially awkward information from each other, she decided to go nuclear. Turning to face me squarely, with her hands on her hips, she asked, "Did you fuck him?"

When I was younger, I would have lied. At thirty years old, what would be the point? If anything, I was proud that I'd managed to end up with such a hot man on my first try. "Yep."

"Good?"

"Mmhmm."

The clicking of the clock hanging on the wall in the kitchen marked the passing of time as we continued to stare, waiting for the other to flinch.

"Well, then. Congrats are in line, I suppose. We'll have to talk about this some more sometime soon, but now I have to get to work. As always, thanks for watching Jeffrey."

"My pleasure. Have a good day at work."

I started prepping my coffee machine.

"Okey-dokey," Jillian said as she backed out the door, her face full of questions.

I'd have to give her real answers eventually, but at that moment, I was full of just as many questions of my own. The first of which was how to talk Evan into that second date that I needed so badly. The quick fuck had been what I'd needed last night, but now that he was gone, I wanted so much more from him.

I knew it was ridiculous to expect anything after just one...well, it wasn't even a date. But why go out looking for someone else, when there was someone perfectly great next door.

5

EVAN

*O*ne and done, I reminded myself as I walked into my messy house. After spending the night in James' much-cleaner house, I had a sudden urge to do something about the chaos that had accumulated in my own place. I started by moving the dishes from the sink to the dishwasher and starting the cycle.

Looking around the rest of my house, I quickly decided that I would need to pace myself. I would have preferred to hire some-one, but thinking about money just reminded me about the car repairs I needed that I probably couldn't afford.

My mind skipped away from that depressing topic, and returned to James.

Everything had happened so fast the night before that I'd barely had a chance to check out his tattoos. I'd have to make sure to examine them more closely next time—

One and done.

Needing some music if I was going to have any chance to get any real cleaning done, I looked around for my laptop before remembering that I had never brought it in when I got home last night. I'd ended up in James' bed before I had even made it home. That meant I must have left it in the car, which meant there was no way I was going to get it until much later in the day. I wasn't going to risk running into James and his sister again until I'd at least had a shower.

Deciding the shower was exactly what I needed, I picked up my clothes and headed upstairs. Since my old water heater was a piece of shit, I started running the water first, giving it plenty of time to warm up. Before throwing my pants into the hamper, I checked to make sure the pockets were empty and found James' credit card. Everything had happened so quickly, but it still seemed like a million years ago that Sean had handed me the card when I mentioned that I lived next door to James. Sean didn't say anything, but had raised his eyebrows high enough. He'd certainly ask me plenty of uncomfortable questions when we both got back to work.

Standing under the flow of hot water, all thoughts of how I'd deal with Sean were washed down the drain. All that was left were memories of James that were all too few and too brief. Even as my muscles relaxed, my dick grew harder.

As amazing as watching his stomach muscles tense as he drove that thick dick of his in and out of my ass had been, and as incredible as it felt to be stretched so fully, I needed more.

I didn't know the shape of his butt, or the smell of his hair, or the feel of his back muscles as my hands wrapped around his neck and he lifted me off the bed and fucked me against the wall with my legs wrapped around his hips.

But I had a decent enough imagination to fantasize in the shower. I could make up the rest. Rather than pretend I wasn't interested, and end up walking around with a hard-on all day, I grabbed my dick and let myself imagine James lowering himself to his knees and taking me in his mouth.

I had plenty of rules about second dates and relationships, but none at all about who I pretended to fuck while jacking off in the privacy of my own house.

James would be stuck on replay for quite a while.

A couple minutes of heavy breathing later, I pounded the shower wall in frustration even as the orgasm swept over me.

Once again it had been too quick, and not enough to satisfy my deeper desires.

I felt old already at twenty-six. My rules had been built up over the years to protect me from all the bad decisions that I frequently made. But I couldn't live like this forever: lonely and frustrated.

Refusing to wallow in my misery, I shut off the water and went off in search of some clothes to clean in, not that I had much that was nice enough that I couldn't clean in it anyway. I settled for an old pair of baggy jeans and yet another t-shirt, and, while I started a load of laundry, tried not to think that I'd have a better chance with men like James if I had some nicer clothes.

He hadn't exactly pushed me away, though...well, once we'd gotten to his place.

Realizing that he *had* rejected me at the club was the splash of cold water I needed on my foolish longings. He was just a straight guy using me to bust his gay cherry to get it out of his system. It wasn't the first time I'd gone through it, and it probably wouldn't be the last.

Considering my "one and done" rule, it wasn't any skin off my back.

I needed to stop thinking about James, and start focusing on the millions of real things that I needed to get done that would actually make my life better. The words felt hollow. The night with James had been better than any in a long time. I hadn't slept so soundly in as long as I could remember. Just having him next to me had been enough to chase away the bad dreams for a night.

The therapist had never been able to do that.

I picked up his credit card from the kitchen table, planning to rush it back over to him and ask him out on a real date. Fate had one minute to give me any good reason to not throw myself at him.

It didn't let me down.

Outside my window I could see James running around in the backyard with the little kid who must have been his nephew. They were playing soccer. The kid could barely dribble the ball, but James kept dramatically falling as if he'd been faked out so badly that he'd lost his balance. With each of James' flops, the kid giggled and kicked the ball toward a tiny soccer net in one corner of the yard. When he finally managed to score, James picked the kid up, set him on his shoulders and carried him for a victory lap around the yard.

It was all too much for me. Way too real.

I couldn't try for a relationship with a guy like that with the likelihood that I'd screw things up and break both of our hearts.

James deserved way better than me.

Returning the credit card would have to wait. I couldn't bring myself to do it when I'd have to look him in the eyes and brush my hand against his. I slid it into an envelope and promised myself I'd drop it off some time after he was gone.

They played soccer for another fifteen minutes before heading back inside.

And rather than cleaning my place, I spent several hours peeking out of my windows, trying to satisfy myself with the few times I saw him pass in front of a window on my side of the house.

It wasn't nearly enough, but I didn't know how to let myself ask for anything more.

6

JAMES

I'd gotten lucky the other day when I'd dropped my nephew off at my sister's. Running late for work, I'd been able to dodge all of her questions...and my own. In the couple of days since then, I'd successfully continued to keep myself in the dark about what to do about Evan.

Waiting for one of my fellow cops to join me at the bagel shop for a regular break during our swing shift, the questions returned.

Evan claimed to not be interested in a relationship, but what would it hurt to ask him out on a date anyway? It wasn't like we'd been friends before, and we hadn't talked since, so there wasn't a friendship to ruin.

I'll ask him.

It sounded confident in my head, but even as I lied to myself, I found a multitude of reasons *not* to ask.

Certain rejection. Uncertainty about how to ask a man out. Confusion about where I'd be willing to go with him.

That last one bothered me the most. I pretended that I didn't care if anyone saw me out with him, but if I really didn't, why hadn't I talked to my sister about Evan again yet? The suggestion that I was avoiding it because there wasn't anything to tell felt hollow. After all, I'd fucked the man. And it was great. And I wanted him again. I'd gushed to my sister over dates based on much less than that.

Fuck.

Fortunately, O'Brian offered a distraction when he flopped into the opposite side of the booth. "What's wrong with kids these days?"

"What happened? Bikes?" There'd been an increase in stolen bicycles recently and no one seemed to know why.

"No. I was walking and my shoe untied. I bent over to tie it, and stumbled. One of those slow motion falls where you keep thinking you're going down any second, and your arms are windmilling. Well, then I finally fell against a garbage can and knocked it over. Then I hear these kids giggling, with their phones pointed at me. They were taking pictures and videos. Fuckers."

When I managed to stop laughing, I said, "Can you imagine the crap we would have done with phones back in our day?"

O'Brian waved my words away. "We were never that bad."

"Says the man that egged the police chief's house twice in high school."

O'Brian laughed at the memory. "He deserved it. The mean fuck wouldn't let Paula date me."

"Whatever helps you sleep at night. Paula was never going to go out with you."

O'Brian and I had been through a lot together. We'd graduated high school a year apart and we ended up going through the Academy together.

"Fuck you," he said. "I don't come around to have you tell me the truth, you know. Because of that you can buy the bagels tonight."

"Fine," I agreed, sliding out of the booth to go place the order. "But I still don't know why we don't just go get donuts instead.

They're all circles that have a million calories. At least donuts taste good."

"Fiber, man. You're getting old and need to keep all that shit from building up inside you," he said, patting my stomach before I could flinch away.

As I walked to the counter, I said, "No idea why Paula didn't want to go out with you, O'Brian."

I ordered our regulars, which they'd already put in bags for us. We definitely needed to mix our breaks up a little bit before we ended up in too big a rut. When I opened my wallet, I noticed that my credit card was missing.

"Hey, O'Brian. Looks like you get to pay. I lost my credit card."

O'Brian grumbled and made fun of me, but didn't say anything that I wouldn't have said to him if the tables were turned. We didn't track money things that closely.

After returning to the table and eating our first bites, O'Brian said, "You heard about that dead kid in the alley the other night, right?"

"Yeah." The Strip had more than its fair share of crime, but rarely murder. Most crimes were limited to theft, drugs, and prostitution. "Anyone figure out what happened?"

O'Brian shook his head and took a sip from his diet soda. "No. Nothing concrete. But it turns out, the kid went to Augusta University. He was a senior. And gay as can be. So, they're checking into whether it was a hate crime, or lovers' quarrel, or if maybe he tried to turn a trick with the wrong man."

"In other words, the detectives don't have a clue, like usual." I hoped I sounded like we were talking about any other random crime in our city. O'Brian's news made me worry about Evan, though. The thought of some guy targeting Evan just for being gay made my blood boil.

O'Brian shrugged. "You know how they work. Turn over every single fucking stone, one at a time, refusing to follow any

hunches and leave us to keep everyone safe while they get
around to putting together their theories."

We both took another bite, knowing it wouldn't do any good
to spend our time complaining about the detectives' methods. We
all knew our roles. We cops would never let them tell us how to
do our job, either, so they certainly weren't going to change their
slow procedures because of us.

The good news was I had a reason to talk to Evan. I could
warn him to be careful. Maybe even offer to protect him. I could
go deep undercover...

"Jimmy, you're not going to believe this. You remember that
girl I told you about the other night?"

"The stripper?" I hid my smile in my coffee cup.

"Fuck you. But, yes, the exotic dancer. She gave me her
number last night."

"36-24-36?"

O'Brian tore off a piece of his bagel and threw it at me. "Why
do I tell you anything?"

"Sorry," I apologized, realizing I'd crossed a line. It was
perfectly fine to make fun of people we *wanted* to date. But it
sounded like O'Brian was getting somewhere with her. I needed
to treat her with some respect in case it actually worked out. "So,
you got her number? That sounds good."

"Yeah, I called her before work and we talked for a while.
We're going out on Friday."

Jealous of his happiness, I lashed out. "You going to stop by
the bank and get singles on your way?"

O'Brian threw the rest of his bagel at me, but laughed. "I don't
know how I'll afford to date her, though. My rent just went up
and I was barely making ends meet before. I'm still recovering
from how much I lost on the Super Bowl. At least I have someone
to go out with, though. When was the last time you got any
action?"

"If you must know, just a couple days ago," I couldn't help

myself from bragging a bit. O'Brian was right. It had been a very long time.

O'Brian leaned toward me. "Who was she?"

"Just someone I met at a club. A DJ there, actually." I tried to stay as close to the truth as possible so I wouldn't contradict myself later when O'Brian made me tell others at the station.

"Nice. Was she wild?"

"Yeah, man. Tats all over and, well, let's just say she needed me so bad that she wasn't interested in foreplay. She practically begged me to get inside."

I felt bad about lying about Evan's gender, but since he wasn't going to give me a chance for another date, it felt harmless enough. Boldly telling myself that I'd have no trouble telling everyone if I ever ended up in a relationship with a man, I tried to shake off the dirty feeling.

"Un. Fucking. Believable." He shifted in his seat, excitedly preparing to ask more questions, but was cut short when his walkie-talkie squawked.

Cindy Walker, our dispatcher, said, "O'Brian, you need to get back to the station and fill out a couple reports before the end of shift."

O'Brian looked at his watch. "Shit." Pressing the button on his walkie-talkie, he said, "Roger that. I'm on my way." Turning his attention back to me, "You coming?"

"No, I just remembered that my credit card might be at the club, so I'm going to head over there and check it out."

"And maybe check out your little minx, huh?"

It wasn't worth denying it. With any luck, Evan would be working and we'd get a chance to talk.

"Which club?" O'Brian asked, snapping his walkie-talkie back into place on his belt.

"The Firehouse."

O'Brian quickly sat back down. "The Firehouse? The gay club? I know that place from our patrols."

Shit.

"They don't have any female DJs, man. I've been in there enough times during our normal walkthroughs that I'm pretty sure of that. Did you...I mean, I can't believe I'm about to ask this, but did you fuck a dude? Was it that main DJ? The one that always wears the hoodies? He's a hell of a DJ, but...I think he has a dick, right? Like an actual penis?"

I could have denied it, but he wouldn't have believed me, he'd still have razzed me about it forever.

Fuck it. There's nothing wrong with sleeping with a man.

"Yeah, that's the one. Evan. And it was fucking great. He did this thing—"

O'Brian held his hands up to shut down my story. "Dude. No, no no. It's cool, but just do your thing. I don't need a blow-by-blow." He blushed at the implication. "You guys like an official thing?"

It didn't really surprise me that O'Brian was so accepting. We'd been through everything together for so long, we'd always have each other's backs for anything important.

I expected the other cops to give me shit, but eventually, even they would be fine.

And having everyone know would give me yet another reason to go after Evan. The quicker the secret got out, the quicker I'd have nothing to hide.

"Not yet. Fingers crossed, though. I'm hoping to talk to him when I check for my credit card."

O'Brian looked thoughtfully out the window. "What do you bring a guy for a date? Flowers? Candy? Wrenches?"

O'Brian always knew how to say the right thing when things got awkward. "I don't know, man. This was my first time and it was more of a hookup."

He slapped the table. "Hey, if it doesn't work out, they have apps for guys like you, you know? I heard about it on the news the other day. Gay guys have like no trouble hooking up anymore. Fucking makes me wish I leaned that way."

When his walkie-talkie squawked again, he jumped to his feet and rushed to the door while yelling into the walkie-talkie. "I'm on my way right now. Just helping Jimmy out with some love stuff."

Thankfully the door shut behind him, silencing the rest of the conversation.

I finished my coffee while wondering at how easily some people could accept something like finding out their best friend was gay. I wasn't even sure how I felt about it yet.

I did know one thing. I wanted to see Evan again, so I finished my bagel and started the walk to The Firehouse, enjoying the breeze and the setting sun, and wondering where my life was taking me.

7

EVAN

I spent several minutes looking at the various containers of oil on the shelf, wondering what the difference between 5W and 10W was. There was no way that I was going to ask Will or Hector. It would turn into an hour-long lecture with them arguing over details that I wouldn't understand anyway. And during the entire process, they'd forget they were supposed to be looking at my car. Neither one of them could multitask worth a shit. They'd both volunteered to stick around after their garage had closed for the night, so I certainly wasn't about to complain that they were taking too long. But that didn't mean that I was going to encourage them to work any more slowly.

From what I understood of their chatter while they were leaned over the opened hood of my car, things didn't look like they were going to go well for my finances, despite their free labor. The two were currently looking at some part they'd pulled out of my car and arguing over it.

When a song on the radio ended and the commercial blasted much louder than the music, I walked across the room to change the channel.

"Whoa!" Hector shouted when he noticed that I'd moved too close to the radio. "This isn't your club, man. You're not the DJ here."

"Yeah," Will agreed. "Touch that dial and I'll send you on your way without even putting this back in." He shook the part at me as if I had any idea about what it was.

Raising my hands high above my head and stepping back slowly and dramatically, I said, "Fine. You win. How much is this repair going to hurt me?"

"Not too bad. A few hundred for the part and a six-pack for me and Hector. We can order it and have it delivered tomorrow."

I shook my head. "Don't bother. I can't afford that right now."

"Shit. Sorry, Evan," Will said. "If you can go down to the junk-yard, you can try pulling a couple and we can try tossing them in and see if they work. I'd recommend not doing much more driving than it takes to get it home, though, until we swap it out. I'm not sure how much longer this one will last, and if it breaks, it could hurt other things and set you back even more."

"Junkyard? Sounds like a fun way to spend the day." Will and Hector both smiled at the sarcasm, but neither volunteered to come with me.

"Hey, you working tonight?" Will asked, mercifully changing the subject. When I nodded, he asked, "There any new guys down there worth me coming to meet?"

With his bulging biceps and pretty face, he had no trouble picking up men despite not always being the best at conversations that didn't involve parts of cars or professional sports teams. For all I knew, that was part of his charm. Will rarely overcompli-cated anything when it came to dating, unlike me and my stupid no-relationships stance.

I shrugged. "Not really." I didn't bother mentioning James because he wouldn't be coming back anytime soon. "But you should come in anyway. I've switched up some songs."

"No shit? About time. Playing anything good yet?" Will joked.

"Nope. But I play it loud and fast," I replied back automatically.

I knew Will's response before he said the words. We'd had this conversation pretty much every time we'd talked about my job. I still couldn't help but smile when he said, "Just like I like to fuck."

If we'd been around a group of guys at the club, that cheesy line would have turned heads. Someone would have noticed Will's chest and arms covered in muscles. Will would have smiled at the attention, and they'd have left the club together shortly after.

Easy as that.

The world wasn't fair most of the time.

Hector tapped me on the shoulder. "Will and I were working out some new beats that you can use, right, Will?"

"Oh yeah. Totally. Check this out."

I was already rolling my eyes when they each grabbed two wrenches and started pounding on the big metal drums full of random fluids. They sounded like drunk woodpeckers attacking a tin roof. When they ignored my pleas to stop, I covered my ears and ran outside to wait for them to stop fooling around and finish up with my car.

The sun had already set, and I needed to get to the club soon, so I decided that if they weren't done in a few minutes I'd just walk to work and pick up the car in the morning. Based on the cost of the part, I figured I might as well get used to walking a little more. At least I lived close enough to The Strip that getting to work wouldn't be a problem if I had to wait a while until the car was repaired.

On the plus side, I wouldn't be able to get within one hundred miles of my parents' house without my car. It would provide the perfect excuse to skip going home for my upcoming birthday. I was already down to just birthdays and Christmas, and that still felt like entirely too many visits.

Things definitely hadn't improved in the years since I'd moved out. I guessed that they'd initially hoped that me being gay was just a phase I'd eventually outgrow, but they were starting to realize the truth. Since I was a stain on their otherwise spotless heterosexual record, they never hesitated to let me know that I had options. Just the other day, they'd reminded me that now that the Republicans had won the election, the vice president might be able to get gay conversion therapy added to health care plans.

What the fuck, Mom?

I shivered at the thought.

Our country would never be cruel enough, right? It's bad enough how popular anti-gay policies are in states like Georgia, but the rest of the country wouldn't let us down.

I couldn't help but feel like a storm was approaching, though, after so many years of tolerance and acceptance spreading across the country.

My phone beeped, dragging me back from the dark thoughts.

It was from Sean.

You give him the credit card? Do it before he accuses me of stealing it!!!

I hadn't. When James was home, I wanted to wait until he was gone. When he was gone, I wanted to wait until he came back home. Either way, I'd become the creepy stalker who knew too much about James' comings and goings.

Comings.

I stifled a giggle, but still blushed remembering the sight of him standing between my legs. My own feet resting against his chest. His dick stretching me to the fullest.

"Looking at some good porn?" Will asked, sneaking up behind me.

Hector shouted from the garage, "Let me see!"

Quickly shoving the phone into my pocket, I shouted back, "You're not even gay, Hector."

He shrugged, "It's still hot."

Will whispered, "He's so gay, he just doesn't know it yet."

I whispered back, "I'm sure you're going to teach him really well some night."

Will laughed, but didn't lose track of his original question. "Was it some new guy?"

"No. Just a text from Sean."

Will would have let it go, but I wanted to tell someone about James. So I told him about the quick, explosive night I'd had with James, and how I'd basically pushed him away because of my own rules about dating. "But it's for the best," I finished. "It was his first time with a guy. You know how that goes?"

"Sure do," Will said. "Hot, sexy, kinky, and dirty. That's the best kind. You get to teach them all the best stuff. So when are you asking him out again?"

I definitely needed to walk to work, and soon, before Will talked me into breaking my rule. "Hey, thanks for looking at the car. I'll stop by in the morning to pick it up. I'll figure out the rest eventually."

"Fine. Hide behind that little protective shell of yours. Anyway, about the car, don't sweat it, man. I'll tow it to your house and leave it in the driveway on my way home."

"You're the best, Will." I turned away when I realized how emotional I was getting over his kind act that I'd never be able to repay.

"I won't even tell you that you'll have to ask him out in exchange. But you should totally ask him out. Your rule is stupid and you deserve to treat yourself better." Will said, already heading back to the garage.

It was hard to believe him when my family hated me so much and I couldn't even afford to keep my car running properly. The only thing that was working for me at all was my job at The Firehouse.

A relationship would just complicate my life.

"Ask him out, pussy!" Hector shouted, pulling down the garage door so he'd have the last word.

As I walked to work, I had plenty of time to try and convince myself to talk to James. By the time I arrived, got yelled at by the owner for being three minutes late, despite there only being five customers in the club, and made my way to the DJ booth, I'd decided that I'd at least see what James thought about seeing where things could go.

When I found my lighter on top of one of my turntables, I let myself believe that it was a sign from above that things were going to get better.

8

EVAN

*I*t was a slow night at the club. Even Trey looked bored as he sipped a red wine, doing his best to look like a moody vampire while hovering near the DJ booth rather than dancing. No matter how much I tried to get him talking, he answered every question with one or two words.

I tried a Hail Mary that had never failed me before. "I've got a fifty-dollar gift card for the MAC website." It was a lie, but fuck it, I needed some kind of entertainment. "You keep saying I need to start wearing some lipstick. Any recommendations?"

"Black," he grumbled before taking another sip.

I was just about to ask him if he was sick when the door opened and the night went from zero to eleven.

James.

In the fucking club.

Wearing his police uniform.

It still had all the tight creases from the dry cleaner. Those creases were strangely hot. There were plenty of ugly cops in Augusta, but James was exactly why people loved a man in uniform. The blue shirt stretched nicely across his broad shoulders and tapered down snugly over his tight abs before diving into his pants.

I wanted to dive in after it.

I had to play it cool, though. I wasn't going to turn into putty just because one glance from him made my legs go weak. It would have, at least, if he'd actually looked at me. Instead he made a beeline for the bar and started chatting with Sean.

Whatever. I have work to do.

I wasn't jealous. It just happened to be the right time of night to play the song that Sean hated and always told me that I should delete from my computer.

I was turning back to talk to Trey to show just how little I cared about what James was doing at the club when he turned, looked at me, and waved. His smile lit the dark room and made me glad I hadn't used my dead car as an excuse to avoid coming to work.

Trey, suddenly chatty, had to tug on my sleeve to get my attention. "You already wrapped around his little finger? Nah, I know that look. You're wrapped around a nice, fat cock." He threw back his head and laughed. "Shit, I didn't expect to see any man make you his little bitch."

When I glared at him, he frowned, as if realizing that being catty wasn't making him feel better, and went back to sipping his drink. I once again wondered if he was sick, but didn't have time to dwell on it because James' presence demanded my careful attention.

Rather than addressing me, though, James asked Trey, "You feeling okay, Trey?" He spent entirely too much time looking up and down Trey's body. "You don't look as glammed up as usual."

Once James said it, it was obvious, but I'd been too distracted making plans to notice that Trey was wearing jeans and a black sweater. That's why he looked so bizarre. He was dressed like some straight guy on business-casual Friday.

Trey nodded, but while answering his eyes danced nervously

around the open dance floor. Something was wrong. "Yeah, baby, I'm perfect. I'm always perfect. Don't you forget it."

James squinted, obviously noticing the lie and trying to figure out what Trey was hiding, and what he could do to help. Despite looking like he wanted to push Trey on the topic, though, he simply said, "Sure. Must've just been the lighting. I can see it now."

Finally after what seemed a million years, James finally turned his attention to me and said, "And there you are."

"Couldn't get me out of your head?" I asked.

Trey rolled his eyes at my corny bravado and turned his back to us, still not making a move toward the dance floor.

"What?" James asked "Oh. Yeah, sorry. I meant that I heard you had my credit card."

At least he looked embarrassed at how his words were crushing my spirit.

"Shit. Right." Reaching into the back pocket where I'd been carrying the card, I realized that I'd, of course, forgotten it. "Damn it. I left it at home. I can drop it off after work, if you'll be there." I wasn't about to apologize. It wasn't my fault I had the stupid card in the first place.

Just as I was about to snarkily ask if that was all he wanted from me, James surprised me. "Perfect. I'll be there. I've been hoping to get a chance to talk." With a wink, he added, "I'll crank up the country tunes, and you can start off by yelling at me, if you're still into that."

His words dizzied me. I'd already started to put up my defenses, expecting a gentle rejection at best. Instead, he crossed the line I'd drawn in the sand, stating pretty fucking clearly that he wasn't going to give up on me easily.

Someone fighting for me was exactly what I needed.

But I knew I'd have to make some kind of move to show him that I was interested in being pursued. The words didn't come right away, though. I thought back to the relationships I'd been in before implementing the one-date rule. They'd never ended well, and I wasn't interested in ending up in the hospital again.

When I didn't even bother to look up from the stain on the carpet next to my feet, James knocked his knuckles on the counter and said, "Loud and clear, man. No sweat. However you want to drop it off is fine."

He stared at me expectantly, waiting for me to stop being a coward.

I took a chance, hoping I wasn't jumping off the wrong cliff. "I'm going to yell at you so hard when I come over."

Risking a look at his face, I was rewarded with a glowing smile. "Yeah, you are. And I'm going to tell you that you techno DJs could learn a thing or two from that big country groove."

I was scrambling for a line to continue our playful banter when Trey groaned. "Oh my God, you two are so lame you might as well buy minivans and go straight. Hold my wine." He handed the glass to James. "I'm going to go piss. Please be done with whatever this shit is by the time I get back."

He didn't leave right away, though. He just looked around the mostly empty club. I wasn't sure if he was looking for an apology, or for me to tell James I wasn't interested, or what.

James wasted no time worrying about it. With his free hand, he grabbed me around the waist and pulled me tight against his body. My eyes sprung open feeling his hardness, but my surprise turned to a laugh when I realized it was his gun.

"I thought you were just happy to see me," I managed to say when he looked at me questioningly.

He didn't bother with any more flirty lines. Towering over me, he leaned down for a kiss. I tilted my head and closed my eyes, ready to throw myself at my very own policeman. The song stopped, but the couple dancers could just hold on a few seconds. I wasn't going to miss the moment.

Just as our lips touched, the squawk of a walkie-talkie interrupted us. James' head snapped toward the sound as he pushed me behind him. I tried to convince myself that it was protectively, but it certainly felt like I was being hidden.

"O'Brian, what the hell are you doing here? Walker's going to ream your ass if you don't get moving." James' body relaxed. He set Trey's glass on the counter and let me go.

Frustrated that I'd been cheated out of a full kiss, I started one of the playlists that I used when I needed a break, and grabbed my lighter and cigarettes. "I'm going out back. I'll see you tonight still?"

"You better."

Doubt crept back in about whether he was looking forward to seeing me or the credit card. "I will. You'll need that credit card, I'm sure."

"Oh yeah. I forgot about that."

James was killing me.

Fuck it. Just believe that he wants you. You're not going to let him go at this point anyway.

James followed me toward the back door. I thought he was planning to join me in the alley until he asked, "So what's up, O'Brian? Need me to set you up with one of the guys? What's your type?"

"Big tits and a wet vagina. You know I'm not into the dudes. I was headed back to the car earlier and heard a fight. Chased a couple guys down the alley out back. Well, I thought they came in here, but I must have lost them. Bastards are lucky it's the end of my shift."

James patted the cop on the shoulder. "You sure you didn't let them go just so you wouldn't have more paperwork to fill out?"

"Shit. Forgot about that. All right, I'm outta here. You'll have to do introductions later," he said, nodding at me.

"Sure," James said. "Bagels tomorrow?"

"Yep. You're paying."

"Then we're getting donuts for once."

I was feeling completely like a third wheel when the other

cop's walkie-talkie squawked again and a voice yelled, "O'Brian. Get over here. I need to watch *How to Get Away with Murder* before I go to bed tonight but I can't leave until you give me that form."

"Coming, coming," O'Brian growled, walking to the front door without another word.

"Where you going?" James asked me when I started toward the back door.

"Smoke break." I shook my hand carrying the cigarettes and lighter at him.

"Hold on. I'll come with you. Whoever he was chasing might be out there still. They clearly didn't come through here. It's a ghost town. We'd have noticed them."

He pushed his way through the door first. His hand dropped down toward his hip, inches from his gun. Every muscle on his body looked ready to pounce if anyone so much as said boo.

All to protect me.

No one ever protects me.

He tugged on the only other door in the alley. It belonged to one of the seven strip clubs on the block. The door didn't open.

"They always keep that door locked," I said. "The dressing room for the dancers is right on the other side of it. None of them ever come out this way. It's safer for them to smoke out front with the bouncer to watch over them and just make sure this door never gets left open."

"It's always dangerous around here? Outside of this new mess?"

"Not really. This alley is normally pretty quiet." I was about to tell him about the one time I'd seen a momma cat teaching her two kittens how to catch a mouse, but the serious expression on his face halted me.

James nodded. "Well, I don't know where they hell they went, but this alley's clear. Whoever O'Brian was chasing must have gotten away or he's just losing his mind.. I'll make sure we increase our patrol around here."

He pulled me back against his body again.

"That gun keeps getting in my way, Officer," I said.

"That's not my gun, but if you keep rubbing against it like that, it might go off."

"Well, we certainly wouldn't want to—"

James interrupted me with the kiss we'd had stolen from us earlier. His lips pressed roughly against mine. There was no hesitation, awkwardness, or shyness. He knew what he wanted, and it was exactly what I wanted, too. I melted into him.

Any thought that I'd had of pushing him away, both in the kiss and the relationship, evaporated as our lips danced together. My hands were pressed against his chest, but I couldn't squeeze anything because of his bulletproof vest.

Before I could lower my hands and squeeze his ass, a bang of metal interrupted us. Once again I was pushed behind James' body. This time it was definitely so he could protect me while confronting the intruder. James shouted, "Hold up your hands!"

Peeking around him, I saw the crazy old man that frequented our alley, looking for food or a place to sleep in the dumpsters. He was leaning with his chest against the wall on the other side of the alley. "Relax, James. He's a regular here."

"You know him?" James asked, looking at the man skeptically.

"Well, not really know, but like I said, he's here a couple nights a week. He's completely harmless."

James nodded, but still turned to the old man. "You see a couple guys run by here? A cop was chasing them?"

The man didn't answer, but the sound of his piss splashing against the wall soon filled the alley.

"You can't just piss out in public, man," James said, pulling away from me. "I can give you a ticket for that."

"James, don't. He doesn't have anywhere to go. He's fine. Let him be. Please?"

I'd spent some time on the streets before getting my shit together, so I knew what it was like for the poor guy. I always tried to do what little I could to help him which normally meant just giving him a cigarette.

When he finished peeing, he started walking toward the street.

"Hey, guy," I called out. When he turned to me, I tossed the entire pack at him. "Keep the pack. I've got more at home."

"Thanks." His raspy voice was like nails on a chalkboard. "No cops."

"Yeah, man," James said. "I got it. You're cool."

"No. No cops were here. No one was. It was just me until you guys. No one else."

When he turned again, neither of us bothered to call him back.

James spoke first. "Man, that guy must be blitzed out of his mind to not have heard O'Brian chasing a couple of punks down the alley. Hey, see you after you're done in there."

With a quick peck on my lips, James walked away to do whatever cops like him did during their shift. I actually found myself looking forward to spending time talking to him about the mundane details of his job.

If I wasn't going to follow my one-date rule, I might as well jump in with both feet.

As I headed back into the club, I took a moment to look around the alley and wonder where two guys could disappear to. It seemed like a dead end to me, but I figured guys like James and O'Brian knew how easy it was for bad guys to disappear into the night. And criminals probably knew every secret passage in the city.

Deciding it wasn't worth worrying about, I opened the door and returned to work.

9

JAMES

*E*van still had that sexy, cocky swagger that I remembered from the other night as he walked across my yard, only this time he was smiling instead of looking like he wanted to fight me. That was definitely an improvement.

I switched the radio from a country channel to a classic rock one, hoping we could find some kind of compromise. I chugged the rest of the beer I had been nursing for the last hour and hurried down the steps to meet him halfway.

"How'd the rest of your shift go? Any other excitement?" I asked.

Evan's hair swung in front of his face as he shook his head. I wanted to reach out and tuck it behind his ears so I could get a chance to touch him again, but he beat me to it.

"It was a pretty boring night. Small crowd like usual for Wednesday, and Trey never did stop being weird. I'm not sure what his deal is. It's not like him to go silent about anything. He normally revels in the attention of any chaos in his life."

"Maybe he's just catching a cold," I offered.

Evan nodded, but looked doubtful. I didn't know what else to say to make him feel better about his friend. After a short silence,

Evan asked, "How'd the rest of *your* night go? Everybody at the station know about us yet?"

"If they did, they didn't tell me...and they would have. Gossip spreads quickly at the station. It'll happen soon enough, I'm sure. It's cool, though. Fuck the haters, right?"

Evan nodded while looking down at our feet.

The mood had turned melancholy. I had no idea how to shake us out of it. A kiss seemed a little too forward when Evan clearly had other things on his mind. I wondered if he was maybe thinking the same about me. Instead of asking, I waved him onto the porch.

While he sat on the porch swing, I hurried into the house to get two sodas. I'd had enough beer while waiting for his shift to end. Another one probably would have just left me more sad and tired anyway.

Before returning to the porch, I shoved a pack of cards into my back pocket just in case I needed something to break the ice.

"Is Coke okay? If not, I've got beer, and water, and could probably make some lemonade."

Evan took the can from my hand and said, "It's fine," and patted the spot next to him on the swing.

We swung back and forth for several minutes, each lost in our own thoughts. I wondered if a relationship with Evan was doomed from the start and if I should just call it off and put us out of our misery. He was clearly uncomfortable with whatever was going on between us and I was about to suggest that we call it a night when he said, "We need something to do, man."

I stood and with a flourish pulled the cards from my back pocket. "Outside or in?"

"Cards? That's almost lame enough to be cool." Evan nodded at the table on the far side of the porch. "It's a nice night and I've been cooped up inside the club."

We both sat at the table. While shuffling the cards I asked, "What do you want to play?"

"Gin Rummy?" he asked.

I nodded. "It's been a while since I've played so you'll have to correct me if I mess up the rules."

I shuffled the deck and held it out for Evan to cut. His hand touched mine for the briefest of moments, but it was enough for me to realize that I couldn't push him away while there was any hope of things working out between us. As I dealt the cards, Evan broke the silence. "Sorry if I'm being too weird. I just don't know what to do in a relationship, you know? I don't have a lot of experience."

I nodded, but didn't say anything that would make me lose track of counting the cards that I was dealing. Once they were dealt, I said, "So we'll take it slow and try to make sure *neither* of us screws it up."

Fortunately, Evan didn't run away at the mention of a relationship. I leaned back in my chair, trying to look relaxed. It was hard to sit still when my heart was racing at the prospect of spending more time with Evan.

Evan surprised me by asking, "So what do you have planned tomorrow? Have any time for a date?"

After how long it had taken us to start talking, I hadn't expected it to leap forward so quickly.

I glanced at my watch. As I picked up my cards and started organizing them, I asked, "You mean today right? I'm actually off for a couple days now. I have to visit my family for a couple hours for dinner tomorrow, but as long as I survive that, I definitely have time to go out afterward."

We picked up and set down cards almost mindlessly while we continued talking. Evan asked, "I thought you got along with your family just fine. It seems like a couple easy hours, isn't it?"

"Normally it is. Tomorrow will be a little rough. It might be at least. Jillian knows about us, remember? She's absolutely not going to let me dodge any questions. Rather than being silent about it, I might as well just come out to Mom and Dad and get that over with, too. It'll be nice to have it over with, but I'm not looking forward to actually doing it."

With his hand resting on a card that he was about to pick up from the table, Evan looked up at me. "Are they going to be okay with all of that? And if they're not, what are you going to do about it?"

I shrugged. "I think it'll be fine. It's just stressful, you know? It seems like a big deal while we're sitting out here so far away from them. I'm sure they'll be okay, but it's still gonna be strange, though. Like more real or something."

Evan moved again and was silent long enough to play his next card before asking in a quiet voice. "Are you having any regrets or second thoughts about us? Or guys at all?"

I shook my head emphatically. I certainly wasn't having second thoughts about Evan. If anything, I wanted more, and faster.

When I didn't say anything, Evan continued. "I knew about me when I was so young. I shoved it in everyone's face whether they were okay with it or not." Evan chuckled. "I was too open probably, but fuck it, right? But I was still just a kid, really. My whole life has been shaped around being gay. I don't know what it would be like to come out as an adult."

"It's all new to me, too, man. If I knew they'd be either happy or mad for sure, I'd be able to prepare myself for that, and probably be fine with whatever happened. It's the uncertainty about how people will treat me that's messing with my head right now."

Evan snorted. "I never had any uncertainty. My parents are way homophobic. They go to the kind of church, well.... There wasn't much chance for us based on that brainwashing."

His parents are lucky I wasn't around back then. I laughed at my thought. *Big talk from the man who's afraid of lunch with his own family.*

I worried the most about my dad. Gay sons always seemed

easier for sisters and moms to deal with, at least on the TV shows. I didn't have much experience outside that.

What would I do if I saw even a hint of disappointment in my dad? He was the guy that taught me to play catch in the backyard. He was the one who encouraged me to stick with football before I started filling out later in high school. He'd always known the right words to inspire me to man up and be more macho.

What is he going to say when he learns his son is gay? Or bi? Or whatever I am these days?

God, how am I going to explain it to them if I can't even explain it to myself?

Evan took a sip from his can before adding, "Besides, Jillian seemed nice enough. And you're certainly nice enough. Kids like that don't come from parents who are assholes. I have the asshole brothers to prove it."

I let myself believe him while we were sitting alone in the safety of my backyard. "Yeah. You're probably right. And the guys at the station will probably be okay, too. They'll be a little strange for a few days, and some of them may never fully embrace it, but I've known most of these guys for too long to think that they're going to kick me to the curb completely. I just wish I'd been the one to get the chance to tell them instead of O'Brian. Although it's probably better if he does. How the hell would I bring that one up?"

I tried to convince myself one last time that everything would be fine. "I just can't wait until today's over. My family will know and it'll be a couple days before I have to deal with the other police. Once I get through the visit with the family I'm sure I'll feel better."

Evan laid down all of his cards and shouted, "Gin Rummy." While I picked up the cards to start shuffling them again, he asked, "Is there anything I can do to help?"

"Call me in sick with my family." I joked.

He laughed and said, "I get it, man. It'll be rough. If you think it'll help, I'd be happy to come along and stand by your side. Offer some moral support or whatever. Give you someone to talk shit with behind their backs if things turn south."

I considered the offer while dealing the next hand. If I came alone, everyone would spend the entire day asking me questions about him, and I wouldn't know the answers. At least if he was there, he could just answer those questions himself. Hell, it would probably make it easier for me to learn more about him, too. "If you're serious, I'd love to have you there."

Looking intently at his cards, he said, "Done deal."

We played cards for a couple more hours. I considered asking him in to spend the night several times as the night passed, but couldn't decide if we were supposed to slow things down if we were going to explore a relationship. Since Evan had all the experience, I'd follow his lead.

It wasn't until Evan yawned a couple of hands later that I remembered that he didn't seem to have a lot of experience with relationships either.

He finally made the decision for us. "I'm going to call it a night and try to get some sleep for the big day. Give me a call an hour before you're ready to leave."

While I gathered the cards, he gave me a quick hug and kiss before he bounced across the backyard toward his house.

With a sigh, I picked up the soda cans and the rest of the cards, and walked back inside my own house, hoping that we could get through the early dating phase very soon so that I could stop sleeping alone.

10

EVAN

*J*ames rang the doorbell once, but didn't wait for an answer before opening the front door and leading me into his parents' house. Everyone was yelling loudly which reminded me of every time I went back to my own house. The chaos was strangely comforting. Maybe if his family was as screwed up as mine it would increase the chance of things working out between the two of us.

It sounded stupid, but I tried to make myself believe it anyway.

James' dad, Nolan Nelson, smiled at us from his recliner, then continued yelling into the phone he had pressed against his ear. A kid, presumably Jeffrey, was yelling from somewhere down the hall that he didn't want to put his pants on. Jillian had clearly heard that argument for too long. Her own voice raised to tell her son that he *would* wear pants at Grandma and Grandpa's house.

Well, it wasn't exactly like my house. Jillian was just tired and frustrated and clearly trying to raise her kid the right way. Jeffrey was probably just tired and hungry. Nolan, from what I could tell, was arguing with a friend about something that had happened in a baseball game the previous night.

They clearly didn't hate each other. Even on the good days with my family, strangers would be hard-pressed to believe that anyone liked anyone else, at least when I was around.

James gently pushed me through all of the noise to the kitchen on the back side of the house. His mom was bent over looking inside the oven while also trying to stir something on the stove.

"Should we help her?" I whispered to James.

He shook his head, silenced me with a finger to his lips, and nodded toward the back door. I followed him, and, seconds after entering his parents' house, found myself alone with James in their backyard. Before James shut the sliding glass door, the fire alarm went off from the smoke coming out of the oven.

The closed sliding door blocked off most of the noise.

James smiled, shaking his head in embarrassment. "Don't worry about them. They'll be fine. Mom's a horrible cook, but refuses any help, and all of them are loud. They'll call us back inside in a little bit and everything will settle down for the most part."

James and I looked around the backyard, neither able to start a conversation. I knew we'd eventually need to figure out how to get better at talking to each other, but decided to go for the easy, physical connection instead.

I stepped forward, closing the gap between us. With our bodies pressed against each other, I looked up into his brown eyes and nibbled on my lip, hoping he'd catch the hint.

He didn't let me down.

Cupping his hand behind my head as I wrapped my hands around his waist, he leaned in for a warm, slow kiss that quickly made me forget anything going on inside the house. His lips were so soft and attentive, that I melted even more into his body. Selfishly, I let myself hope that the visit would be short so we could get back to one of our places to fool around more properly before our real date.

I opened my eyes to ask him if he had any ideas where he wanted to go, but when I noticed his eyes were already open and staring at me, I said, "Eww. You're an open-eyed kisser? That's creepy, man."

James leaned his head back away from me, a questioning look on his face. "Is it? I never really thought about it, I guess."

I shrugged. "Yeah, it kinda is. I'm standing here with my eyes closed, all vulnerable and focused on our kiss. And who knows what you're looking at? The house next door? A squirrel on the fence? How messy my hair is?"

"Maybe it is a little strange. But I swear I was only looking at you. It's like I'm afraid that you're going to disappear if I close my eyes too long."

I groaned and shoved him away. "God man, that was corny," I said playfully even though the words made me feel great.

Stepping toward me, James leaned down for another kiss. Just as our lips touched, the door slid open, and someone cleared their throat.

We quickly pulled away from each other and turned to face the door, but rather than separating from me entirely, James' giant hand wrapped around mine as if promising to protect me from anything that was about to happen.

Nolan said, "So the rumors are true." Rather than looking upset at seeing his son holding another man's hand, though, he held his own out to shake mine. "I'm sure James has drilled all of our names into your head. It's a nervous habit. He does it with anyone he introduces to us. He never does the same for us, though."

Hearing the implied question, I answered, "Evan. Pleased to meet you, sir."

"No sirs or ma'am in this house, please. Nolan and Maggie will do just fine. So what do you do, Evan?"

Nolan's eye contact was a little overwhelming, and I almost

laughed when I realized how similar it was to James kissing with his eyes open.

Before I could answer, James said, "Come on, Dad. You just met the guy. Take it a little easy on him so you don't scare him away, okay?"

James' voice was playful, but I thought I could hear a slight tension. His dad held his hands up defensively. It felt like they were both going through their well-practiced roles.

Wanting to make sure that Nolan liked me since I thought it might help his family accept learning that James was gay, I said, "It's okay, James. Sir, I mean Nolan, I'm a DJ. Down at The Firehouse, one of the clubs on The Strip."

Maggie, perhaps with a little too much excitement in her voice, nearly squealed, "Oh, that gay club. I've heard it's great for dancing." She spun in a circle with her grandson in her arms, and finished by dipping him. The boy giggled, the argument over his pants long since forgotten.

James groaned. "Jesus Christ, Mom. What do you know about the only gay club in town?"

In a perfectly friendly tone, but without backing down one inch, she replied, "Up until earlier this morning, I would've said the same to you. Looks like we're all full of surprises, aren't we?"

None of us had a reply for that.

Maggie handed Jeffrey back to Jillian. Smoothing out imaginary wrinkles on her apron, Maggie said, "Shit. That came out all wrong. We're excited for you, James. We just don't know exactly how we're supposed to show it. You, too, Evan. You seem like a fine young man, and I hope my James is taking good care of you."

I squeezed James' hand, hoping it would help him relax. James had no idea how lucky he was to have parents that seemed to only care about his happiness.

I was certainly jealous.

"No worries, Maggie," I said. "The sooner we get it all out on the table, the sooner we can all be perfectly comfortable around each other. Ask me anything, I'm an open book."

Nolan, Maggie, and Jillian all started asking different questions at the same time. Even James was able to laugh at that, which went a long way toward clearing any stress.

Jeffrey took advantage of the quiet moment to get in the next question. "Do you like Elmo?" he asked.

"Who?" I asked wondering if I had misheard him.

"Elmo, Elmo, Elmo," he squealed. "Come inside. I'll show you."

Jillian picked up her son, and told him, "No TV until after lunch."

"How about you show me after dinner, okay?" I offered, figuring winning over the kid wouldn't hurt me one bit.

"Tell us about your family," Nolan said, wrapping an arm over Maggie's shoulder and pulling her against his side. Without missing a beat, she tipped her head against his shoulder while continuing to look at me with a friendly smile on her face.

After a couple of seconds of me stumbling around, trying to get out of talking about my family, James swooped in and saved me.

"Hey, Jillian. I thought you said Rick was going out of town?"

She sighed dramatically and said, "He is. That convention thing he told me about, remember? That's why Jeffrey is here today."

"That's what I thought," James said, clearly lying about being surprised. "But while we were driving over here, I saw him walking into one of the bars on The Strip. You don't think he was lying to you, do you?"

James' voice made it clear that he certainly thought Rick was lying.

"What the fuck? Shit. What the hell?" She corrected the profanity after a quick glance at her son. Jillian turned and stormed back into the house, pulling her phone from her back pocket.

Nolan and Maggie followed.

"Don't call him," Nolan shouted. "The less you, or Jeffrey, see of Rick, the better off we all are."

Alone again on the porch, James winked at me. "Rick's good for exactly one thing. Getting everybody in my family pissed at him so they forget about me. Good thing I saw that slimy bastard during the drive over."

"Thanks," I said. "Your family is so nice, though. I just got caught off-guard. I barely like to think about my family, much less talk about them. I'll have to find some way to make it up to you later."

Placing himself squarely in front of me, James said, "Another kiss would go a long way toward squaring everything up as far as I'm concerned."

While we kissed again on the back porch, any worries about my own family drifted away. I risked a quick peek while James' tongue explored mine. His eyes were closed. He looked so peaceful and happy that I was able to understand the attraction of being able to see the other man while kissing.

But James caught me in the act. "Hey, eyes shut, mister."

He lightly bit my lip as punishment.

Instead of making me feel bad about peeking, the bite just made me want to earn another. But with his family waiting inside, we could only grab each other's hands and walk back inside to join them for dinner.

11

EVAN

*W*e stopped at The Firehouse after dinner so we could have a drink and figure out what we wanted to do next. The DJ working that night sucked. He was a new guy, but I doubted he'd make it through the summer.

James didn't seem to agree. He was singing along with the Donna Summer's song. At first I thought he was just fucking with me, but as his head continued to bob in rhythm to the music, I finally rolled my eyes and let it go.

Country music and disco. I should have asked him about his taste in music before starting to fall for him.

James was leaning against the edge of his stool alongside the tall table. He pulled me against his lap and laid his arms over my shoulders. His hands beat the rhythm of the song on my chest.

I had to admit that the man had rhythm. I was looking forward to getting him home later and having him show me all the other moves he might know too.

"Listen to that beat, Evan, how could you possibly not like this song?"

Held tightly against his body in the mostly empty club, I forced myself to stop hating the music enough to enjoy the moment. His strong hands rubbing my stomach made it easier to do. Ever so slowly they were sliding down to my bellybutton and then down inside my jeans, and then lightly with one fingertip stroking the side of my cock which sprang to attention at the bold move.

I flinched, but James didn't move an inch when Sean said, "Here's your drinks. If you're planning on handjobs, please take it out to the alley."

James' finger moved just far enough away that it wasn't touching my dick anymore, but stayed down my pants and against my skin.

If I wasn't so set on us not being the kind of guys who only ever fucked, and never talked or went out in public, I would have begged him, on my knees if I had to, to take me home.

Sean sat down across from us. Within a few seconds, our table was surrounded as Topper, the bouncer; Owen, the bartender; and some guy I recognized as the drummer from one of the local bands joined us.

Regrettably, James removed his hand from my pants as the crowd gathered.

Owen and Sean, both reliant on tip money, were complaining about the lack of visitors to the bar over the last few days.

I was having trouble paying attention to the details, though, because James' lips kept sucking on my neck just below my ear. It wasn't until I felt his body stiffen and his head snap up as he started to pay attention to my friends that I was able to hear what they were saying.

"Don't play, Liam," Sean said to the drummer. "You know it's because they were gay. Three men? All gay? It's a hate-crime spree for sure."

Liam shook his head. "I'm not saying it's not. I'm just saying that we don't know. For all we know it could just be some crazy psycho who happens to be targeting people in the same little area. It could be a coincidence that they were all gay just because we have a higher percentage of gay guys that hang out around here because of this club."

Sean waved off what he clearly thought was a ridiculous statement with the back of his hand. "Get out of here. Believe whatever you want if it helps you sleep at night, I guess. But pay attention when you're out in the streets."

Owen nodded in agreement. Even Liam seemed to agree with that too. "Of course. No point being stupid."

James' voice, already so close to my ear, seemed like thunder when he asked, "What are you guys talking about? I've only heard about the one death, and I patrol in this area pretty regularly."

Owen laughed. "Imagine that, guys. A cop doesn't know about the recent crimes against us gays in town. Big shocker."

I had to stop myself from nodding my agreement with the rest of the group. It would be a hard habit not to immediately assume that all cops were idiots.

James wasn't about to be ignored, though. "There was a kid killed in the alley a couple blocks over a few days back. I heard rumor that he was gay. What else happened?"

Everyone seemed to realize what it meant for me to be dating a cop. All of their old fears and biases suddenly made them mute after years of bragging about how tough they'd be if they ever had the chance to give a cop a piece of their mind.

Since no one clearly was going to speak up, I pointed at them all one by one and said, "Tell him what's going on. We always talk shit about how the cops never give us any protection, and now there's one right here, asking what he can do to help, and you're all going to clam up? I better not hear any of you whining if you don't start talking now."

Liam pointed back at me and said, "How long have you two been together? Are you sure he's here to help? Don't go being stupid just because he's a good lay."

Sean piped up before I even had a chance to yell back. "Shut up, Liam. Not everyone's out to get you. I've talked to James enough times to know he's one of the good guys." Turning his attention back to James, he continued, "We don't really know that much, to be honest. You know about the guy that got shot. He was gay. Like most of the college kids that come around here, none of us really knew much about him. The other two guys are both okay other than some bumps and bruises, like the first guy, they were just college kids. I don't think any of us even know any of their names. But when three guys who have all been seen in this place in the last couple weeks all get beat up or even killed, you don't have to be a mathematician to add that up."

James banged his fist against the table. "Shit. I agree with everything you're saying, but, if that's all you have, I'll have to agree with Liam. It might be that, or it might be some other connection. Or just shit coincidence. Is there any other info?"

Owen laughed, and leaned back with his hands across his chest. "Oh, big shock. The man in blue, who just decided that he's gay the other day, has trouble believing that hate crimes exist."

I spun and put a hand on James' chest just to make sure he didn't overreact to Owen's words. I knew I would have.

James didn't though. Instead he said, "I'm not saying it isn't a hate crime. I'm just saying that as a cop, I gotta make sure I don't blind myself to what could really be happening just because of what I think might be happening. There are other problems down here on The Strip. Prostitution, drugs, I've even heard rumors that there's been some point shaving going on at the college. So I have to look at all the facts. All three were gay. Fine. Is it possible they all played on the football team? Were they somehow mixed up in one of the other crime scenes around here? See what I mean. I have to keep an open mind about every-thing. You guys, though, *should* treat it as a hate crime and take whatever precautions you need to. Buddy system to the car, that kind of stuff. Keep your eyes open and report anything that looks suspicious, okay?" With that last word, he locked his eyes on mine, making sure that I understood his concern.

It was strange feeling like the police were on my side for once. Normally, if I had to choose between the cops, and the bastard criminals in the town, I would choose to make myself as invisible as possible and let them fight each other. It was comforting to know that someone as protective as James was on my side. Especially since he might be able to make sure the rest of the police had our backs, too.

I nodded and gave him a quick kiss.

The other guys around the table started to relax as the tension that had been building disappeared.

Sean hopped up from his stool and stretched his back.

Before any of us could say anything else, another guy walked up to our table. I'd never seen him before. And I would have remembered. Tall and strong with a face that wore a few scars as trophies of all the fights he'd survived, and a Mohawk at least five inches tall, the man would have stood out anywhere. Instead of the confident powerful voice I expected, he mumbled something to us.

Sean said, "Don't be afraid of us, dear. We don't bite. Well, sometimes we do, but we know how to make it feel good. What are you looking for?"

The man cleared his throat. "Luca. Looking for a man named Luca. I heard he works somewhere around here. You know him?"

We all looked at each other and shrugged.

Owen answered the stranger. "Don't know a Luca. If you want to stick around and have a couple of drinks and tell us a little more about him, maybe we'll be able to help you figure something out."

The man shook his head, raised his hand in a quick wave, and backed away from the table. He was out the front door a few seconds later.

"Damn," Owen said. "I wouldn't have minded kicking him out of my bed tomorrow morning."

We all laughed.

"Strange dude," Liam said.

Everyone except James agreed. James' eyes were still on the front door. I couldn't tell if James was watching him because he thought the man was hot or if he thought the man was suspicious.

I wasn't going to be *that* guy and show how jealous his attention on the other man was making me, though.

When one song ended and another began, James jumped to his feet and dragged me to the dance floor before I even recognized the tune. A few seconds later all of us were in the middle of the dance floor dancing to "YMCA."

I'd never danced to disco music in my life, but dammit, waving my hands in the air with James and my friends that night made me understand that not all disco music was horrible.

12

JAMES

*D*ancing to "YMCA" with my boyfriend and the other men in the club made me feel about as gay as anything else I'd done in the last few days. Any hesitations that I might have had about being seen on a date with a man were gone. It felt great to be free of the weight that I didn't even know I'd been carrying around.

After the song finished, I wanted to dance to another, but Evan said he needed a smoke. I hated that he smoked, but I wasn't going to be *that* guy.

The two of us walked to the back door hand-in-hand, but our laughter was cut short when we made our way outside and saw who was leaning against the wall on the other side of the alley.

"Trey!" Evan screamed, rushing toward Trey.

Trey flinched away, but not before I saw the blood streaming down his face from a cut above his eye. He was still on his feet, though. That was a good sign.

While Evan tried to persuade Trey to let him see his injuries, I took a second to scan the alley to make sure whoever had committed the crime wasn't hiding out waiting to finish what they'd started.

After the conversation about the crime spree we'd had inside the club, and the two guys who'd disappeared on O'Brian, it was impossible not to see Trey's beating as a targeted attack.

If they even think about touching Evan...

Other than us, though, the alley was empty. Something felt wrong about that. I'd seen plenty of beatings during my time on the force. Most of them were between rival gangs or drug deals gone bad, but the victim never walked away with just one cut to show for it.

Heading back to Trey and Evan, I tried to get control of the situation. They were both crying. Trey looked mostly pissed and almost embarrassed that we were seeing him in such a condition.

Evan, on the other hand, was showing some signs of shock. His eyes were wide and his breathing quick and shallow. His efforts to clean Trey's face had resulted mostly in smooshing the blood around.

Taking both of Evan's hands in mine and making sure he was looking me in the eyes rather than off into space, I calmly said, "Evan, I need you to do me a favor. I need you to make a phone call. Call 9-1-1 and tell them what happened. Do you think you can do that?"

"I don't need no fucking cops," Trey said. Glaring at me, he added, "None of them. Dig?"

Understanding why a black, gay man would hate cops didn't make me an angel. It still hurt whenever I saw how little some people trusted me just because of my job. "Sure, tough guy. I get you. Thing is, there was a crime here, and I'm going to make sure it gets reported. This is bigger than just you. We've already had one gay man die around here." I glanced at Evan. He was fumbling with his phone, still trying to dial the number with his shaking hands. "I'm going to make sure there isn't another."

Trey laughed. "Sure, Officer. You go ahead and try to crack that case. Chase that trail up whatever trees you want. Just don't walk too far out on those limbs because," he paused long enough to look up and down my body and lick his lips, "you're a solid man who might just break that branch and the problem might be at the trunk."

"What the fuck are you talking about?" I shouted, wondering if Trey had a concussion.

Evan waved at us to shut up. He'd finally managed to get through to someone. He nodded several times as if the person on the other end could see him before he finally managed to say, "Okay. One sec."

He wobbled unsteadily.

I worried that he was about to pass out, but he took a deep breath and said, "I'd like to report a... Well, that we need an ambulance, I guess. My friend was beaten. Hate crime. My boyfriend says to send cops. He's one himself. You might know him. James? He's a great guy—" He nodded as the operator cut him off. "Yes. Sorry. One, ma'am. Lots of cuts." He looked closely at Trey. "Actually, just one cut. Trey, you going to be okay?"

I breathed out a sigh of relief as Evan seemed to be pulling himself back together.

Trey was looking at his face in the mirror on some makeup compact thing that he must have carried in a pocket. "Those motherfuckers busted my eye, that's all. It'll swell shut, but that's why God gave us two, right? Still think I'm pretty, copper?"

I swatted Trey's hand away when he reached for my chest.

"Stop it," Evan snapped at me as he slid his phone into the pouch pocket on his hoodie. "Trey got hurt, James."

"You're yelling at me? He's the one who—"

Evan motioned for me to shut up. Using the sleeve of his hoodie, Evan was able to clean Trey's face much more success-fully. His free hand rubbed Trey's arm, comfortingly.

I continued being useless and growing frustrated. I was the cop. I was supposed to keep things like this from happening. Instead I'd been inside dancing with Evan and having a good time while an innocent man was being beaten just a few feet away.

We needed to get to the bottom of this and arrest whoever was committing these crimes against the gay men of the city. I needed to make sure the chief understood how serious this was.

Shocked at realizing what it felt like to belong to the group needing the help for the first time ever, I suddenly understood why guys like Trey treated me the way they sometimes did.

Trey looked ready to yell something else at me again, but the sound of the police-car siren interrupted him.

"Sooey!" Trey shouted at the two officers as they stepped out of the car. "I think you guys have the wrong alley. I heard the free donuts were a block that way." He pointed with his middle finger.

"Hey, O'Brian. Franklin." I shook their hands. "I think everything's okay here. The perp is gone. Trey, did you see anything useful while you were getting beaten up? Like hair color, skin color, T-shirt logo?"

Trey seemed to have decided to stare at O'Brian to see if he could get him to flinch. O'Brian was not backing down one bit, though, which was out of character for O'Brian who was usually fairly gentle with even the worst of suspects, and even nicer to the victims.

"No, see, the thing is I was out here peeing because the john inside was full."

I hadn't seen Trey inside the club since we'd arrived. I made a mental note to talk to the guys in the club to see if they'd seen him at all, but didn't say anything out loud. Trey clearly wasn't going to say anything useful on purpose, but sometimes little things slipped out if guys like Trey talked long enough.

"I was peeing so long that I got tired and closed my eyes and then bam!" Evan flinched when Trey shouted that last word. "The bastard snuck up and clocked me."

He shook his head and went silent.

"You need to learn some manners," I told Trey, pissed off

because he was being such a jackass. "We're the ones that will find the asshole. And talking about cops like that isn't going to do anything to help, man. Just tell us what you know so we can have a better chance of stopping these attacks."

Trey smiled and zipped his lips. "My momma always said that if you don't have anything nice to say, you're probably talking to a cop."

I didn't know how to reply to that.

The other cops shifted in annoyance, and O'Brian said. "We'll file a report to get this logged, James, but don't hold your breath. Especially if the victim himself isn't going to talk to us."

"Yeah, gotcha." I frowned at Trey, who was already walking back toward the street, and added, "Log the time and location and hope someone else calls in something useful, I guess."

Trey flipped us off one last time before disappearing around the corner.

O'Brian grunted and turned his attention back to me. "Fun guy. Anyway, want to help us out with some of that paperwork by answering some questions?"

"Sure. Fire away."

Franklin asked, "Who was the victim?"

"Trey."

"Last name?"

I looked at Evan and raised my eyebrows.

He shrugged. "Just Trey. Like Cher and Madonna."

Franklin snorted, but wrote the name in a notepad. "Did you see anybody else?"

"No," I said. "I checked, but there was no one but Trey when we came out."

"Where were you right beforehand? And how'd you end up in this alley?"

"Inside. Dancing." I blushed realizing how quickly we were heading into my own personal life. "Evan wanted to smoke, so we came outside." They knew I didn't smoke, but I didn't offer any explanation about why I'd come out, too. Questions from cops had never made me so uncomfortable.

O'Brian did push the subject.

"Did you call in the incident right away, and is there any witness to confirm all that?"

I bristled at being treated like a suspect. "What the hell is going on here? What aren't you guys telling me?"

The two of them looked at each other, and then Franklin said, "We've heard some rumors about this alley. Drug deals. Trey is probably mixed up in it. We don't know your friend at all, so we we just need to cover our bases. Besides, you're practically a regular here, right?"

"Are you fucking kidding me?" I yelled at O'Brian. I wanted to smash his face for outing me without my permission, but knew it wasn't the time or place. "I answered all your questions. Go do some fucking police work."

"Trey isn't a dealer," Evan said, his voice growing louder. "He's strange, but he isn't involved in any of this. He was a victim here tonight."

I stepped away from the two idiots with my hands clenched into fists, and walked past Evan, who turned and followed me. Just inside the club, I stopped and turned back to Evan. Any thoughts of it being a coincidence that the gay men of the city kept ending up beaten or worse were gone. "I need to talk to Trey and find out what he knows. You and I know that these are all hate crimes. We gotta get this shit figured out fast." I nodded toward the door. "They'll...I mean, we'll do our best, but with staffing levels the way they are it's hard enough to get our jobs done most days. It'll be hard to make it as urgent of a priority as it should be without more victims, if you know what I mean." Looking closely at Evan, I added, "I don't want any more victims."

I felt like shit talking about my fellow policemen that way, but they'd asked for it with the shitty way they'd treated me. It felt like they were saying that because I'd slept with another man, I wasn't one of them anymore.

Screw O'Brian and his big fucking mouth for spreading the news.

Frustrated at not being able to do anything, I kicked the wall. Unsolved crimes were nothing new. But not understanding what was happening, and knowing that my lack of knowledge meant that Evan would be at risk each time he went to work made my blood boil.

If only Trey would talk.

I kicked the wall again. "Trey's such an asshole."

"Relax, James. He was attacked and is scared. He might not show it, but he can be vulnerable just like anyone else. He didn't mean anything by it, I'm sure. Trey's one of the good guys even if he might not seem it at times. Whenever some new guy ends up on the streets because his family kicked him out or he lost his job or whatever, Trey always helps him get back upon his feet. Just let it go. For me."

The intensity in Evan's voice surprised me. Trey had clearly made an impression on him. If Evan trusted him, I told myself that I should give Trey some benefit of the doubt. I nodded and pulled Evan in for a hug. "Okay," I agreed. "No fighting."

Evan reached up and patted my cheek to let his hand trail down over my chest. His gentle touch snapped what was left of my anger, leaving me with a ton of unused adrenaline.

With a big exhale of air, I looked him in the eyes.

He smiled and said. "I agree to one thing, though. Trey has to know something. But he isn't going to tell you. In his mind, you're one of them. Let me talk to him alone and see what I can find out. He'll be more chatty off the record."

"So we're in this together?" I asked wrapping my arms around the small of his back and pulling him against my body.

He ground himself against my crotch. "I'm not going anywhere. I'm horny as hell, though. I know I shouldn't be right now, but I don't want to go back in there and talk to them tonight. There's nothing they can do." Sliding his hand up inside my shirt and rubbing it against my bare skin until he reached my nipple and gave it a little pinch, he finally said, "I just want you, right now. Take me home and keep me safe."

I nodded, but playfully asked, "Keep you safe? Or fuck you?"

With a devilish smile, he said, "Both."

Rather than risking the guys trying to get us back on the dance floor, we escaped out the back door again and hurried away from the club.

13

EVAN

*B*y the time I locked the deadbolt on my door, James had already removed his shirt, shoes, and socks, and was tugging on his pants and underwear. I turned around just in time to see his big cock spring free and bounce like a diving board.

I was ready to jump right in and test the water, but I also wanted to keep some small amount of pride. Moving slowly, I started undressing myself rather than dropping to my knees and taking James into my mouth.

There'd be plenty of time for that.

While slowly folding my shirt, and trying to look casual, I asked, "So what happens now?"

James used both hands to point down to his erection.

"No, silly. I mean, yes, but that wasn't what I was talking about. What happens with these crimes? Do you guys go out there and start looking for fingerprints and shit?"

Apparently growing bored with how long I was taking to get undressed, James started to slowly stroke himself while he said, "Not me or even my department. For us street cops, it'll mostly just mean more of us on patrol in the area each night. Most of the time just having more of us cops around will encourage whoever's doing this to lay low for a while. That gives the detectives time to do things like look for clues, and interview suspects and the victims and try to put a case together."

While listening I'd removed my pants, folded them, and was setting them on top of my shirt when I said. "So all of us are really still at risk if whoever's doing this decides they don't give a shit about your increased foot traffic, right?"

James shrugged. "The fact of the matter is, a bad guy who isn't afraid of the police can strike anytime, anywhere. But the more of us that are around, the better chance of noticing something and minimizing the damage. The key for you and all the others is to play it safe. Buddy systems are more effective than you'd think. Use them. Especially after dark."

I didn't bother folding my underwear. All this talk of the dangers of the city was overwhelming. I seemed to have two choices: cower or live for the moment. And at that moment, there was a gorgeous hunk standing naked in my living room, teasing his dick to keep it hard until I could take care of it for him.

I chose living for the moment.

Dramatically throwing my boxers over my shoulder, I rushed into his arms. As we kissed, our dicks rubbed against each other's body. The feel of him against me wiped any thought of what was happening outside of my house from my mind.

With one hand, James gently pushed my upper body far enough away and lowered himself by squatting just enough that he could reach down between us and grab both of our dicks with his other hand. I rested my hands on his shoulders to hold my balance as he stroked our cocks with one hand. Using his thumb, he teased the beads of cum from the tips of our dicks, eventually using his palm to spread over the shafts, too. The sensation was overwhelming.

I was surprised at how quickly James had learned the trick, considering he hadn't been with another man before me.

My breathing grew louder, but I wasn't ready for an orgasm yet. It was my turn to push him away. "Sit down on the couch."

He complied with a smile. With his legs spread wide and his giant cock raised up against his stomach, and that hungry look in his face, he looked powerful and masculine.

I dropped down between his legs and set to work. Grabbing his shaft with one hand, and his balls with the other, I took the rest of him in my mouth, excited at the pleasant stretch of my lips. I wanted to tell him how much I enjoyed us being together, but knew the words would just come out all mumbled if I tried. Instead I moved up and down the shaft letting my tongue trail along the vein and hoped that said enough.

He answered wordlessly by grabbing my hair and holding my head in place. I got the message. He wasn't looking for a long leisurely blowjob.

With my head held in place, he started thrusting with his hips, pushing himself deeper into my mouth each time.

I tried to time my own hand movements with his thrusts to increase the pleasure, hoping that was what he wanted. All I could think about were his needs and how I could help him achieve those.

It was so much different than with any of my other lovers where I usually focused too much on my own desires.

Is this what a relationship is supposed to be like? Was enjoying being face-fucked just because of the joy it brought my lover what love was really all about?

My thoughts strayed from the more vague questions to the more immediate situation as James continued searching for his release. His grunts and profanities helped me know when he needed my grip tighter or for one of my fingers to press more firmly against his asshole.

Eventually his entire body went rigid in the split second before he yelled, "Fuck!" and exploded in my mouth. I swallowed quickly to make sure none of it escaped.

I want it all because it is mine.

I blushed at the ridiculous thought.

"Whoa. That was amazing," James said between heavy breaths as his body recovered. "What can I do for you?"

"Turnabout's fair play," I said, hoping I sounded more mysterious than lame.

But I didn't want him to do anything as if it were some kind of favor. I wanted to take what I needed just like he'd done. After only a split-second of hesitation, I jumped onto the couch and stood straddling his body.

His eyes went wide, but he didn't push me away or back away from the challenge. With one hand cupping my ass, he pulled me closer and licked the tip of my dick. "You taste great, Evan."

I groaned in ecstasy.

James smiled briefly before leaning in and taking me into his mouth. Doing my best to not rush, I kept my body very still as his tongue alternated between exploring the underside of my shaft and flicking repeatedly, very lightly, against the tip.

I realized that I'd let him take over, but damn. For a man who hadn't given a blowjob before, he sure caught on fast. He was already doing a better job than most of the guys I'd been with. I couldn't wait until he got some more practice.

That last thought briefly made me lose my focus.

Are we only in this for the sex?

We still hadn't even had much of a real date yet. Hanging out with friends at the club where I worked didn't feel real enough to count.

The thought didn't linger once James started sucking like he meant it, rather than just teasing me. I couldn't tell if his moans were real or something he was doing to drive me wild, but the effect was the same.

It wasn't long before I passed the point of no return.

I needed something to grab onto or I was going to fall off the couch, but there wasn't anything near enough other than James.

When I grabbed the top of his head, he pulled away, and while still pumping my dick with his strong fingers, asked, "Everything okay up—"

The orgasm shook me as I came in an arc over his shoulder and onto the couch.

James caught me off guard when he said, "Whoa. That was just like in the videos."

I fell onto the couch beside him, laughing and trying to catch my breath.

"What?" he asked with fake indignity. I could hear the smile in his tone, though.

"You're crazy," I said and threaded my fingers through his.

"Well, I guess it wasn't *just* like the videos. Those guys usually take it in the face, right?"

"Oh my God. Shut up before I kick you out of the house."

He covered his mouth with his free hand and mumbled something indecipherable.

"That's better," I said. "Let's cuddle for five minutes. Then I'll clean up this mess and show you my bed."

14

JAMES

*I*t felt like my body was moving through molasses. Evan was half a block ahead of me, walking with his headphones on. Two men with their faces buried in ski masks approached him from the opposite direction. Evan didn't notice them, though, because he was looking down at his phone typing a text, probably to me.

I tried to shout but no words came out of my mouth.

I tried to run, but while my legs moved, my body didn't go anywhere.

The two men reached Evan.

Evan looked up at the last moment and flinched when he realized how close the other men were.

My heart raced. I couldn't help him. I was worthless.

He tried to politely step to the side to let them pass, but they charged forward, each grabbed an arm, and carried him into the narrow gap between two buildings.

I was finally able to scream, but my body still wouldn't move. I shouted obscenities and threatened to murder the strangers if they so much as laid a hand on my Evan.

One of the evil fucks popped his head around the corner, looked right at me, and laughed. "We'll take good care of him. Real good care."

The laughter was still ringing in my ears while somebody shoved my back. Evan's voice rang out through the night, calmly saying, "James. Wake up. It's just a dream."

———

*M*y hands tapped out a fast beat on the steering wheel. After the nightmare, I insisted that we get Evan's car fixed when I woke up. I couldn't be there to protect him all the time, and he needed a safe way to get himself around town. I knew he'd still have to walk from parking lots to the building, but I refused to dwell on that.

Instead, I focused on what I could do.

It's not enough.

Evan eventually agreed to let me help him out and called his mechanic friend. Will had an opening, but not until after lunch. The morning had passed too slowly while we'd tried to distract ourselves by doing laundry and playing cards.

A car honked and then passed me and then Evan in one move.

Evan had himself convinced that if he drove faster than five miles per hour, the car would blow up. Maybe he was right, but with only a couple of hours until I had to leave for work, the sooner we got to Will's shop and the car was fixed, the sooner I could relax a little bit.

I liked telling myself that I would have done the same for any person in the city, but knew I was going beyond the normal call of my police duty with Evan, and just hoped he didn't think I was trying to trap him into anything with the offer.

But things had clearly been developing between the two of us beyond just a quick hookup. I was anxious to put the menace of the city's attacks behind us so we could get back to focusing on the fun parts of our relationship. All the worrying for his safety was stressing me out.

The previous night had been a perfect example of the teeter-totter of emotions that I was wrestling with. Between seeing Trey beaten and projecting my own worry of the same happening to Evan, and the incredible night fucking with hours of cuddling between, I couldn't imagine things being much better or much worse.

Can I survive much more of this?

I wasn't looking forward to being away from Evan while I went to work, but at least while I was there I could try to do something to help figure out what was going on with the attacks, and hopefully help put them to an end.

Shutting down the voice that said there would always be more bad guys out in the world, I turned on my turn signal and followed Evan into the parking lot.

Will and Hector, the other mechanic in the shop, quickly dove into their work. There was a lull in this part of the afternoon so they wanted to get the work done before any real customers started arriving again.

Evan and I huddled together against a wall, watching, and staying out of the way, but not out of the conversation.

"Will, we missed you at the club last night. You should come down after work." Evan said.

Will stood up from where he had been leaning over the hood of the car and stretched his back. "I was thinking about it. Might as well check out the fresh meat."

Evan shook his head. "Pickings are slim, but you should come anyway and say hi to the guys. Business sucks right now. You heard about Trey right?"

Will set down his socket wrench and pulled a part out of the car.

It made me happy to know that Will and Hector were Evan's friends. I knew nothing about car repairs and always worried about getting scammed.

"Of course," Will said. "Bunch of bullshit going on down

there on The Strip these days. No wonder business sucks." Will set the part on the rolling table next to him, pointed a finger at me, and said, "You guys make any arrests yet?"

I bristled at the inference that us cops didn't know what we were doing, but tried not to let it show. Hanging around with Evan and his friends had been eye-opening. I was probably nearly as pissed as all of them that we cops hadn't done anything useful yet.

Before I had a chance to go into some long-winded explanation about the difficulty of solving these kinds of crimes, Hector, returning from getting a soda from the vending machine, said, "They've got shit. But I heard some news." Looking me square in the eyes, he said, "A guy I know told me something."

Oh great.

Police are used to hearing about the mythical guy someone knows. It's never a reliable witness.

Hector must not have seen me roll my eyes, because he continued without pause. "Someone came up to my friend and offered him money. Couple hundred. Told him all he had to do was jump a guy in an alley and shoot the gun the guy had. The guy said he could shoot it up into the sky or into the mark's head. He didn't give a shit."

My ears perked up. It was most likely just a rumor, nothing more real than people believing Batman roaming the streets or fat guys dropping down chimneys to deliver presents, but it never helped to ignore potential evidence either.

Gather it all and make sense of it later.

Hector opened his soda can and took a sip before continuing. "My friend turned it down, of course. Not that he'd do it anyway, but this guy felt really seedy. He got the vibe that a cop was trying to set him up. Someone's doing this shit, though. Maybe someone did take the money. Maybe not. Maybe it wasn't a police setup, at all. Maybe it's just a cop that's killing you gay guys."

"Fuck you," I yelled before regaining my composure. Evan

had grabbed my arm to keep me from lunging at Hector. I patted Evan's hand to let him know that I wouldn't do anything rash. "Sorry, Hector. But we cops don't do that stuff, man."

Hector laughed. "Sure, they don't. All the cops around here are squeaky clean, of course. But that friend of mine, he's a good kid. He had no reason to make up that story."

Hector was protecting his source as fiercely as I would have protected mine...if I'd had one. I didn't know much about Hector, but he certainly didn't seem like the kind of guy who mixed with trouble.

At least in the brief interaction I'd had with him.

Profiling is a bitch, but every cop gets their hunches from somewhere. My hunch was saying that Hector's story had enough truth to it that I shouldn't discount it entirely.

"James, you gotta go," Evan said.

I glanced at my watch and saw that I was going to be late for work. I hated leaving Evan here without knowing that his car was going to be okay.

Will must have noticed my hesitance. Or maybe just wanted me to leave so things could get back to normal.

"We'll have Evan set up in no time. But if not, I'll take him to the club in my car. It'll give me a chance to have a couple drinks and do a little dancing, too."

I nodded. It was certainly better than Evan walking himself to work alone. After giving Evan a much-too-short kiss, I turned back to Will. "No drinking and driving, right?"

Will rolled his eyes and didn't bother replying. Evan shoved me out of the garage. "Don't worry, Dad. I'll get an Uber if Will has more than a couple."

I walked out of the garage, but not before I heard Hector, Will and Evan all laughing at my overly dramatic worry. I blushed realizing how foolish I'd sounded. I needed to get to work and get myself good and distracted for a few hours.

15

EVAN

On the way to work, I decided to stop at Trey's and get that conversation started. I had to ring the doorbell three times before Trey finally opened the door to his apartment. Without even saying hello, he turned and shuffled back to his couch. He was wearing a food-stained robe and based on how much chest and leg I could see because of how loosely he'd tied the robe, nothing else.

The house smelled like shit. No, death. Like the door hadn't been opened in months. It was dark as hell, too.

"Hey, man." I tried to sound excited to see him, but couldn't even manage a follow-up to my greeting.

I sat down in the chair next to the couch. When I realized that Trey wasn't about to spark the conversation, I said, "How have you been?"

"Shitty."

He wasn't planning to go into details, which was not normal. Trey could talk for hours about anything that caused him the tiniest slight. He'd sounded out of character in the alley, but I'd been able to explain that based on him having just been attacked.

But thinking back, he'd sounded odd the time I'd seen him before that, too.

It was hard to focus because of the funky staleness of the air. I hopped back to my feet. I knew that I was fidgeting, but like usual, was unable to do anything about it. Instead of sitting back down, I wandered to a window, trying to keep my movements as casual and steady as possible.

Trey groaned when I drew the curtains to brighten the room and pulled the window open to let in some fresh air.

"Hey, dick. Shut those," Trey protested.

He didn't move or complain further when I ignored his weak demand.

Rather than returning to the couch, I stayed near the window. Turning back to face Trey, I saw that he'd bought a new TV. The last time I'd visited, he'd still had the old-fashioned little cube-shaped TV that he'd had in his bedroom growing up. He'd always said there was no point in upgrading when he was never home anyway.

"Nice TV. Planning on staying home more often?"

"Yep."

One of the big mysteries and points of gossip around the club is where Trey got his money. No one had ever heard him mention a real job. There were plenty of rumors of rich benefactors who paid for his things in return for sex, but if he *was* pimping himself out, it seemed like he'd be able to afford a nicer place to live.

I'd always assumed that he'd received some kind of inheritance that was big enough to escape the rat race but not big enough to live like a queen.

"Oh, speakers and a PlayStation, too? That must have cost a fortune. Where'd you get the cash?"

Trey looked me squarely in the eyes. It looked like a real effort. "I saved my pennies, bitch. Stop smoking and you can get some nice shit, too."

God, I could use a smoke right now.

"Listen, I just came over to make sure you were okay after last night. Is there anything I can do?" I looked around at the discarded microwaveable frozen food trays he'd left around the living room. "Maybe help you clean up around here?"

"Leave it. It doesn't matter. Enough about my sad ass. Tell me about you and your hot cop."

Happy to move on to a more pleasant conversation, I leaned back against the wall. I pulled my cigarettes from my pocket, preparing to tell a story before realizing that I was inside someone's house. I didn't smoke inside. After shoving the pack back down in my pocket, I said, "Great. Everything I could ask for, and more than I deserve."

I should do something special for him.

"Big dick?"

I rolled my eyes. Trey always focused on the important things. "Stop being an ass, but it's perfect." We'd fucked three times last night, each time better than the last. I was surprised I could even walk. "Better than perfect. More importantly, he's nice, you know? Not a selfish prick like most guys."

How many guys have called me the same over the years?

Unable to keep my body still any longer, I bounced around the room gathering the garbage while I talked. "I met his family already and they're all sweethearts. Like something out of a sitcom."

"What'd he think about yours?"

"Hasn't happened yet, and it won't if I can avoid it. They'd certainly scare him off." I tossed the mess I'd gathered into the garbage can in the kitchen.

"The nut doesn't fall far from the tree, does it?"

Trey was trying to sucker me into a fight, but I wasn't going to bite. "You know it. Oh, and he helped me pay for my car repairs just because he's worried about me walking until the cops catch whoever is behind the attacks."

"What'd that cost you? You better be using a condom."

I snorted. Those two sentences captured the essence of Trey. Able to needle raw nerves with the best of them, but still a protective mother hen in his own right.

"Always, Trey. But it didn't cost anything. I'll just pay him back when I get the money."

Despite thinking I sounded confident, his words had shaken me a little.

What if he does expect something?

Not the sex. I would willingly have given him whatever he asked for in bed.

But what if he expected a commitment? Monogamy? Marriage?

I shook the crazy thoughts from my head and focused on the new question Trey was asking.

"Where are these so-called experts looking for the bad guys? Or are they just eating donuts in alleys?"

I stomped my foot defensively. "Cops don't just sit around eating donuts in the real world, you know? But I'm not sure where they are focusing other than downtown. James hasn't told me much."

"Do they have any suspects yet? Are they increasing cop patrols? Any FBI?"

"No suspects. James said he expected more cops around. FBI? Why would the FBI get involved?"

"Don't ask me, cop lover. I'm just making small talk. You're the one that came to my house. It just seems like if you know anything, you should let us friends of yours know so we can protect ourselves. Not all of us have cops ready to take a bullet for us."

"Jesus Christ, Trey. You need to take a chill pill. Cops are the good guys. James would do anything to protect you or Sean or even the asshole that runs the smoke shop because that's literally his job."

It sounds good, but do I really know that?

We'd all heard stories of corrupt cops. It was certainly possible that James was one. It didn't feel right, but my instincts weren't necessarily the best barometer. I'd been with plenty of jerks in my life. Hell, that was the reason for the no-relationship rule in the first place.

"Just keep your eyes open, Evan," Trey said, sounding more like mother hen than needling bully. "No one is willing to be a superhero without a reason, and a paycheck isn't enough, especially on a cop's salary. Mark my words, the crimes aren't happening without some police support. I've heard things about a couple. One named Rick, and that O'Brian from the alley last night. Just shadows of rumors, but still. Although if your cop is springing for car repairs and who knows what else, maybe he has some supplemental income, if you know what I mean."

"Fuck you. You're not going to make me go jumping at shadows just because it's fun for you to watch everyone else be miserable."

I fled the apartment and slammed the door behind me before saying anything else.

As I stormed through the parking lot, I remembered that I'd meant to pick Trey's brain for leads. Somehow he'd turned the tables on me and rather than using the meeting to my advantage, I'd run away. While I lit a cigarette, I considered going back inside, but was afraid Trey would trick me into assuming the worst about James, and I'd already been shaken enough for one afternoon.

Go to work. Everything gets better when I'm playing my music.

16

JAMES

*D*espite the stereotype, I loved sitting around eating donuts, I just wished I had better company to share the sugary goodness with.

O'Brian, despite his regular insistence of the superiority of bagels, was dunking his third chocolate donut in his coffee. I couldn't stop watching as he leaned over to take a bite. There was no way he wasn't going to drip coffee onto his shirt before our break was over.

Rick had barely said a word, which would have been fine if he wasn't watching every move the cute, young waitress made. Thank God that Jillian wasn't with that idiot anymore. He'd been a creep back then, too.

Not much had changed, but at least most of it happened without my knowledge. I'd lost track of which girl he was currently dating which was more than okay with me.

I closed my eyes and imagined O'Brian and Rick being replaced by Evan. He was feeding me little nibbles of donuts, and dipping his finger in the icing and letting me suck it off. When I opened my eyes, though, the swap still hadn't happened. Since

I'd tried to magically teleport the men three times already, I gave up and finished my donut.

The waitress finished wiping down a table and disappeared into the kitchen.

"I'd like to dunk my donut in her milk," Rick said, still staring at the swinging door.

"What the fuck does that mean?" I asked, adding a chuckle to soften the attack.

"Yeah, that's pretty lame," O'Brian agreed while dabbing his shirt with a napkin.

Damn. I missed it.

"It means that I'd stick my long john into her..." unable to finish his donut analogy, he ended with, "her vagina."

"You're going to ask her first, right?" I asked, only half-joking.

"Nah, man. She's gonna ask me. You'll see. That girl's a freak. She's got those eyes."

"Shut up before I arrest you for...well, just for being an ass." I said, glancing at my phone for any excuse to cut short this fucked-up break.

Rick, thinking I was impressed with his banter, smiled, waggled his eyebrows, and ran his fingers through his hair.

I shuddered at the thought of anyone asking for Rick to touch her.

Why did you hook up with this fuck up, Jillian?

I was just about to leave when Rick asked O'Brian, "So, did you hear anything about that body you found?"

O'Brian shivered, and shook his head.

"What body?" I asked.

Rick patted O'Brian's shoulder conspiratorially. "Another guy got shot last night. O'Brian found him, but no leads, of course. I mean, it was O'Brian that found him, so what do you expect?"

O'Brian shook off Rick's hand. "You didn't find shit either, asshole."

"True, but we didn't know we had a serial situation back then.

And my guy had been dead for hours. If he'd been alive when I arrived, I would have made him talk."

"Whoa," I said to O'Brian. "He died after you arrived? Are you okay?"

Things like that can scar cops and lead them to alcohol.

He shrugged and tried to smile, but his eyes were dead for a second before he pulled himself together and shoved Rick, nearly toppling him out of the booth.

Rick laughed and flipped O'Brian off.

It felt like I was in the lunchroom at high school again. Everything was such a macho show of one-upmanship that a real conversation couldn't possibly occur.

Rick smiled that creepy smile that said he'd thought of something cruel that he thought was witty. And his eyes had settled on me. Shifting toward the edge of my booth, I prepared to leave, but Rick was not going to let himself be denied.

"Well, I heard one thing. He was a faggot, too."

My body froze, every muscle tense. Blood pounded in my ears.

When I didn't respond, Rick dug his knife in deeper. "So, recently all of us have found gay guys who'd been attacked. Two of them dead. One alive. I think we know who the gay cop is? Although, O'Brian's victim almost lived, so maybe he's not as straight as he pretends."

"Too much, man," I said. "Filter some of that shit before it comes out of your mouth." Completely over any sympathy I might have felt for O'Brian, I asked, "And what the fuck, man? Why'd you have to run off and tell everyone about me and Evan?"

O'Brian's eyes went wide. "I didn't. I only told Franklin. And that was an accident."

"Chillax, Jimmy." Rick put his arm up on the back of the booth cushion, clearly enjoying the chat. "O'Brian didn't say shit. I wasn't even sure until just now."

"Then how'd you—"

"I'm a cop. I find things out, unlike you putzes. So a bunch of gay guys are getting bumped off on The Strip. This wouldn't happen if there wasn't that club down there luring them all into one spot."

"Filter." I growled. Trying to change the subject, I said. "They're all gay, but are there any other connections?"

"The college?" O'Brian asked. "The guy I found went to school there. So did the first one."

"It can't be the college because Trey doesn't go there," I said. "Unless he has some other connection to the school, I guess. I'll talk to Evan about it. So if this is a hate crime, who would want to kill gay men? We should start that list."

Rick laughed. "Do you ever get out of the house? Half this city would be on that list."

O'Brian shook his head. "It isn't that bad, but Rick does make a point. There are plenty of haters out there. It could be anyone."

Rick rubbed his face with both hands. "Oh my God, listening to you guys talk is killing me. If I leave you two alone, do you promise not to blow each other right here in the donut shop?" Before I could protest, he held up a hand to stop my verbal assault. "I'm just fucking with you. I don't give a shit who you fuck as long as you stay away from my girlfriend...well, I guess I don't have to worry about that anymore."

I wasn't about to explain that being bisexual meant that I could still be interested in his girlfriend. I certainly wasn't going to go after Rick's sloppy seconds.

Rick hopped to his feet and clapped his hands. "Right, then. Off to catch some bad guys while you two make sure no one robs the donut shop."

O'Brian turned his attention to me. He looked about to apologize about something, but couldn't find the words. What did he have to apologize for if he hadn't outed me to Rick, though?

Not interested in hearing any more from O'Brian, I said

goodbye and headed to the counter to order a dozen donuts to go. After my shift, I planned on popping in at The Firehouse to check on Evan, and thought my new friends there might like the treat.

17

EVAN

*E*ven though he'd been able to get the car fixed in time, Will still showed up at The Firehouse. He was completely ignoring me, though. With Trey still not back out in the real world and Owen and Sean both busy serving drinks to the surprisingly large crowd, I was so bored.

Maybe I need a change of venue?

But the closest place worth considering was in Atlanta. I would have to sell my house if I was going to go that route for more than just a temporary gig.

Looking for some kind of distraction, I started playing a game on my phone, but got annoyed when it kept showing me ads between each level.

I was excited when a text interrupted the game until I saw that it wasn't from James. It was Mom, asking me to confirm that I was coming home in the morning to spend my birthday weekend at their house. I couldn't imagine why they would want me there unless they had some kind of intervention planned.

Refusing to answer right away, I sat on my stool. My heel tapped the ground at a much faster beat than the wild techno song I was playing. Even the thought of a conversation with my mom set my nerves on edge.

They all deserved for me to bring James home and make out with him right in their living room, but I wouldn't subject James to the torture that was my family.

After deleting my third angry reply before hitting send, I shoved my phone back in my pocket. She could wait.

Maybe I should just go and get it over with for another few months.

Getting away from The Strip didn't sound like the worst idea with all the recent crimes, and it wasn't like James had bothered to invite me anywhere. If I went, at least I wouldn'tbe sitting around my house all weekend hoping that James would decide to ask me to do something.

I was just silencing the voice that said that I could ask him instead of waiting when I looked up and saw James walk into the club like some slow-motion movie star. The way he managed to wear a simple pair of jeans and a white tank top and still attract everyone's attention was uncanny. But I certainly couldn't pull my eyes away either.

That glowing smile and playful twinkle in his eyes. Those shoulders and arms covered in tattoos that I still hadn't properly explored yet. The tight jeans, barely able to contain the treat that waited inside. Even those silly cowboy boots that he wore with no sense of irony. Everything about him was perfect.

He looked great in his uniform, but he looked amazing in his regular clothes.

And even better naked.

I was mesmerized to the point I couldn't stop staring until the crowd started booing when the song ended and I failed to start the next.

He waved at me with one hand. A box of some sort was pinned against his side with the other.

A present for me? Does he somehow know my birthday is coming?

James hurried through the crowd straight to my DJ booth and

held out the plain white box, saying, "Just a little something for you."

"Aww. You didn't have to." But it was certainly nice that he had. My excitement was short-lived, though. Disappointment replaced it when I opened the box and saw the donuts inside. At least Trey wasn't there to point out that he had been right about all cops loving donuts.

But that's all he was right about.

Still, I frowned at the donuts. "Thanks. I mean, a sweater would have been nice, too, but thanks."

"Have one," James said, fortunately not noticing the snark in my tone. After all, he couldn't have actually known it was my birthday.

He was facing the dance floor now and dancing in place, kind of shifting back and forth with his hands held up in front of his chest.

"I just ate," I lied. "You look like an accountant when you dance like that, you dork." I had no idea why I was being so crabby, but I blamed it on Trey.

Fortunately, James didn't call me out on it. He went into some Saturday Night Fever moves. He had the grace to pull it off, but I didn't have the perkiness to appreciate it.

"So, thanks for stopping by—"

"Yeah, sure. Hey, do you mind if I go dance for a few minutes? I had a crappy shift and need to burn off some frustrations."

"Knock yourself out," I mumbled, turning my attention to my laptop, and hoping I would get my head out of my ass by the time he came back.

"I'll be back in a couple songs."

Before I could respond, he rushed out onto the dance floor.

Along the way, he grabbed Sean and pulled him along in his wake. As the two danced, a circle opened around them. James' body moved faster and smoother than it had any right to move. Unlike when I watched him dance to YMCA the other night, he actually moved around the dance floor with Sean, spinning and dipping him perfectly in beat with the song which I was pretty sure he had never heard before.

Sean was flirting it up, knowing that the attention would help with tips from other guys later, but he made sure to make eye contact with me as if to let me know there was nothing happening between them. He didn't need to do anything to convince me, though. James was constantly glancing my way and pretending to kiss me from across the room.

His silly attention actually made me smile. At least I didn't have to worry about being jealous over Sean. I wished that James was twirling me around the dance floor like that, but knew that if I tried to cut in, I'd just end up stepping all over James' feet. I was better off bobbing my head in the DJ booth and making plans to kiss James when he returned.

Over at the bar, Owen was wiping the counter and frowning. I looked around to see if someone was bothering him, but the bar looked pretty quiet. The frown seemed to deepen when he looked at James and Sean.

I did not know what to make of that. Owen clearly liked both of them and *had* to be able to tell that James was not making a move on Sean right in front of me.

Thinking back to how my mom's text had bothered me just a few minutes earlier, I decided that Owen was probably just having a bad day, too. Who wasn't recently? Fortunately, James did not give me much of a chance to dwell on it.

Standing in the middle of the dance floor, he waved for me to join him.

I shook my head and pointed at my equipment, happy to have an excuse to not embarrass myself in front of the crowd. It always blew everyone's mind that I could be a good DJ but also a terrible dancer.

Still dancing, he slowly made his way through the dance floor back over to me, his hips jerking to the beat hypnotically.

As he got closer, I wiped my hands on my pants. James still made my heart flutter and my hands sweat more than any high-school crush had ever managed.

"Have plans for tomorrow? I want to take you out somewhere nice." he asked.

I thought of my mom's text. I really *did* need to get back home eventually. As stupid as it sounded, it still felt like I owed them a couple of trips a year and my birthday seemed like a completely obvious one.

Even as my head started to nod, though, I said, "Nope."

James laughed. "Should I listen to your head or your mouth?"

"Which one takes better care of you?"

James bounded up the stairs and pressed me against the wooden railing on the far side of the booth. I bent backward against his unrelenting passion as he dipped me over the wall and pressed his lips against mine.

I quickly lost track of the crowd, the room, or even the music as I gave myself over to him. My hand rubbed his cheek, feeling the roughness of his end-of-the-day stubble.

Why would I ever think of leaving his side to visit my shitty family? James was all I needed.

The railing wiggled as James tipped me back further.

"Whoa. Hold on. I think this rail's gonna break." I said.

James pulled me back upright and tucked my loose hair behind my ear. I needed more.

The crowd was cheering about something. It took me a few seconds to realize that the music had long since stopped, and everyone in the club had turned their attention to James and me. We'd been kissing for a couple minutes, and I hadn't even noticed the time passing.

Blushing, I pulled myself back up, smoothed out my hoodie, and approached the microphone. "Sorry about that." Whistles and catcalls from several of the men filled the room. "Why don't I just get another song started for you guys?"

James' warm breath tickled the back of my neck as he growled from behind me. "Stop by after work."

Just as quickly as he had arrived, he hopped down from the booth, gave Sean a quick hug, waved at Owen, and marched out the front door, leaving me alone with the crowd and my music.

After selecting a song and sitting down on my stool, I let myself wonder where James would be taking me and what I would need to wear.

Shit. I hope it isn't somewhere too fancy. I don't have clothes for anything like that.

Sean brought me a soda. "Really? That song? You've got it bad. Congratulations." With a smile, Sean sashayed back through the bar, looking for his next tip.

Turning my attention to the laptop, I saw that I had picked the sappiest pop love song that I owned. Instead of feeling bad about it, I took a deep breath and told myself that I deserved someone like James, for once, and just hoped I would be able to make him feel the same.

I considered sending my mom a text, rejecting her invitation, but decided I did not want her reply to ruin my fun.

Most of the night passed in a series of daydreams and awkward shifting to hide the occasional erection when the daydreams were too good.

18

EVAN

*O*wen had volunteered to walk me to my car, but I'd turned him down so I could spend a little time after work on some new lighting effects around the DJ booth that I wanted to tweak. The lights were bright as fuck and the first time I'd tried to use them, they'd blinded the people on the dance floor.

I wound up being happy about not making him wait when it ended up taking an hour to get them redirected to angles where they'd still dramatically accent the music while maybe not flashing in too many people's eyes. I didn't think I had them right yet, but I was tired, and sick of messing with them.

Still, despite that, I was in a very good mood as I walked to the parking garage at the end of the block. I was heading to see James again.

My mind wandered to James and what he'd be wearing when he opened the door. Hopefully, those very thin blue pajama pants I'd seen sitting folded on his dresser the other night. No shirt. Just muscles, tattoos, and a dick that couldn't possibly be contained by any fabric.

I'd press my body against him, nip at his nipples until they hardened, and then suck on them until I felt his dick harden against my body.

Reminding myself to pay attention to my surroundings didn't help. Even the thought of James' body was distracting. I did pick up my pace, but only because I wanted to feel James' body, and have him tell me more about his day.

Hell, I even wanted to tell him thanks for giving me an excuse to avoid my parents that weekend.

I stopped short in the middle of the row of the second floor of the parking garage when I saw that someone had slashed my tires.

Alone in the empty garage, I felt more terrified than I'd ever felt before. Goosebumps rose on my arms as I spun to make sure no one was sneaking up behind me. After taking two steps toward the car, I stopped again, realizing that I only had one spare tire and two were flat for sure. What if whoever did it was hiding behind, under, or in the car.

Nope. I'm not going to be the dumbass to fall for that. The car is useless to me. I'll come back for it later.

I was down the ramp to the ground floor and out of the garage before I slowed to get my bearings.

The shortest route home would take me past the alley behind The Firehouse.

Fuck that!

As I looked up and down the block, I swore I saw millions of alleys. Alleys inside of alleys. I couldn't walk home in any direction without passing all of them.

Maybe not all of them, but too many.

I needed help.

Ducking down behind a hedge that lined the parking garage, I called James.

No answer.

Fuck. Where are you?

I climbed out from behind the hedge and held myself tall,

convincing myself that I'd be fine. I'd walked home so many times without any issues.

Tonight won't be any—

A gunshot exploded behind me. I dove to the ground with my hands over my head before realizing that bullets don't stop just because the person they are aimed at surrenders.

When I heard the squeal of tires, I realized that it had just been a car backfiring.

Feeling stupid, I stood and wiped off the pebbles that had stuck to my palms. Without pausing to let doubt settle back in, I started walking to my left, and turned down a side street that would take me away from The Strip and avoid the alley behind The Firehouse.

My heart rate had finally settled down. I kept my pace brisk, but my mind was able to focus on how much bullshit it was that I couldn't feel safe just walking home. The world had some bad monsters. I knew that, but I never really believed they lived so close to me.

Sure, assholes who shouted, "Fag," or even picked fights existed almost anywhere. But people who would actually kill a man just for being gay? That was bullshit.

A few blocks passed uneventfully and my normal love of walking in the cool summer night air returned. I checked my phone, but James hadn't called or texted. Figuring he was asleep and I was going to be fine, I didn't bother him.

Instead, I imagined letting myself into his house, climbing up the stairs, and stripping while I walked down the hallway to his bedroom. He'd be asleep on his back. I'd straddle his chest and tease his lips with my dick until he woke, smiled, and opened his mouth. His tongue would feel—

The streetlight I was walking under popped and the street went dark, sending shivers down my body.

I've gotta stop jumping at shadows. I'm a grown man who can walk himself home from work.

A dog barked, convincing me that I really couldn't. I flinched and ran before seeing that he was locked up in the backyard of a nearby house.

Why am I noticing all of these things tonight? Surely, they happen pretty much any night.

Wondering what it would take to convince me that the world was safe again, I pushed onward, knowing that the only escape from the fear would be in James' arms.

The world was too cruel. Well, at least around The Strip.

A cop siren sounded in the distance.

"Catch the bastard," I whispered angrily into the night.

That's what the world needed. Cops like James keeping the evil at bay. Guys like him could help all of us find the strength to endure the terrors of the night.

I was being melodramatic, but fuck it. It had been a rough week, but I'd reached James' house, so everything would soon be fine. The lights were all off, but I heard country music again from the back porch.

The thought of how comforting his country music was made me smile at how quickly things had been changing in my life. Sure, plenty of it was bad, but James more than balanced it all out.

Walking between our two houses, I tried to think up a cocky insult for his bad taste in music, but couldn't. I just wanted him to hold me. I was tired of dealing with life alone.

We'd have to do something about the tires tomorrow, but after that we'd still have time for that real date that James was planning.

Someone touched my face.

I screamed and kicked out at the unseen attacker. My arms flailed into the darkness of the night.

It was like fighting a ghost, though. There was no one there, but he kept touching my chest and scratching at my face. It didn't matter which direction I turned, the attacks were all around me.

Just when I started to notice that the punches were not hurting me at all, I was lifted off the ground.

"James. Help!" I screamed while kicking back at the beast that had grabbed me.

"Shhh. Relax," James whispered calmly into my ear. "I've got you."

When I calmed and he set me down, I spun and wrapped my arms around him, fighting like hell to stop the tears that threatened to flow.

"Who the fuck was that? Why can't you cops even keep your own houses safe?" I snapped.

"Dude, you were just caught in the branches. It's dark as hell on this side of the house. Come on. Let's get you inside and make sure you didn't get any cuts."

I didn't offer any resistance when he pressed his hand against my back and lead me to his porch.

Everything would be okay now. James would protect me.

19

JAMES

*E*van had looked so fragile all tangled up in the branches. I wanted to hold him in my arms and protect him from anyone who might want to hurt him.

We needed some real information to leak about the crime spree and the only possible lead seemed to hinge on whether Trey would talk. He had to know something. No matter how much Evan wanted to protect his friend, I thought it was time to bring Trey in for questioning.

That's a problem for when I get back to work, though.

The stairs creaked as we walked up to my back porch. Poor Evan flinched at the first one and grabbed my hand. After that, he made it the rest of the way without any problem.

On the porch, Evan turned to face me. He was standing so close that I imagined I could feel the heat of his body, but it was probably just my own desire ramping up at the hope of fucking him again. I'd imagined a dozen different ways to take him while waiting for his shift to end, and decided that I wanted to try something a little different from just hopping into bed. I planned to fuck him from behind with him bent over the bathroom sink so we could watch each other in the mirror.

I wasn't sure now with how spooked he still looked after his battle with the tree. I worked really hard not to smirk at the thought of him flailing at the branches. Lord knew I'd been spooked by sillier stuff in the dark.

Before I worked up the nerve to make the suggestion, Evan asked, "Where are you taking me tomorrow for our big date? Will I need a tie and dress shoes?"

The curveball caught me off guard. I stammered as I replied. "What? No. Nothing like that. Unless that's what you want?"

Evan laughed. "I don't care, man. Anywhere is fine with me as long as you're there. I don't have a lot of formal clothes, though."

I kissed his forehead as I relaxed. "Just a little Mexican place across the river in South Carolina. And then I was thinking about ice cream afterward. Now that you mention it, though, ties might be fun. I can loan you one if you need it. But no fancy shoes. We'll call it sexy casual."

Evan lightly punched my stomach. "You're such a dork. Thanks for the invitation, by the way. You're saving me from going back to my family for the weekend."

"What's going on back there?"

"They wanted to see me for my birthday. But, shit, I hate going home. This will be a million times better."

"What? You have to go home, Evan. I get the reluctance, but once a year for your mom on your birthday is okay. I'll go with you like you did for me."

"No," Evan said simply, pulling away from me and sitting on the porch swing.

Staying right where I was standing, but unable to stop from raising my voice, I said, "Why not? It can't be so bad back there that one visit with me will be too much. And then you'll have it out of the way. Jesus, you saw my family. It was horrible. But we'll get through it. Don't be a pussy."

Evan rushed to me and poked his finger against my chest. "My family. My rules. Okay?"

I worked really hard to make sure I didn't start yelling. "Sorry, Evan, but that's bullshit. We're in this together, right? That means we talk this shit out and do what *we* want and need. It isn't a dictatorship."

"Listen, James." All I heard was the snap of my first name as it turned it into the deepest of profanities. "We can talk through plenty of issues and work them out like rational fucking men. But not my family. They are *not* up for discussion. Clear?"

Real honest-to-God crickets marked the passage of time as we stared each other down, waiting to see who would flinch first.

I finally realized that I really didn't know enough about that relationship to tell him that he needed to endure whatever real pain they might cause just so that I could satisfy my curiosity of meeting them.

"Shit, of course. I just know how much better I felt after you met my family." Evan looked ready to tear my head off. I raised my voice to cut him short. "But, I get it. Just because that was good for me doesn't mean it would be good for you. Consider the topic dropped."

Evan nodded, but didn't seem happy or even relieved. He paced back and forth on the porch, bouncing on his toes a little with each step as if gravity was just barely able to contain his energy and keep him bound to Earth.

"Fuck!" he finally shouted. "Why'd you have to be a dick about this and then back down right away? Now I'm all pissed off and don't even have anyone to fight anymore."

Covering my mouth to suppress a laugh, I nodded. "Sorry. Should we just go our separate ways tonight to cool off and regroup in the morning?"

"Hell, yeah, I'm going home. Asshole. The only thing worse than the bullshit was getting all nice afterward. Now my head is all dizzy and I don't know what to think."

I'd fucked up and we were both suffering because of it. Poor Evan had taken the brunt of it, but, well, hell. I'd been ready to fuck and my balls ached at the thought of Evan leaving me alone for the night.

I needed to find a way to keep him around. A way that would make him feel better, too.

"See you later, prick." Evan's tirade seemed to be cooling despite his words. He'd stopped pacing and still hadn't made a move to leave, but he certainly wouldn't stay long if I didn't say something to make staying worth his while.

"My handcuffs," I blurted out, imagining him bound to my headboard and at my mercy while I did anything and everything to pleasure him to make up for my mistake.

Evan nodded.

Thank God.

When Evan said, "Your ass is going to look so good when I cuff you to the bed," though, my blood went cold. The thought of him taking charge in the foul mood he was in terrified me...and curiously, excited me, too.

"Let's go do this," I agreed.

Evan laughed. "Your ass is mine, James."

As odd as it sounded, those words calmed me. I thought I'd be perfectly happy with Evan owning my ass for the night.

20

JAMES

*J*esus fucking Christ, what kind of man agrees to be handcuffed and fucked by his boyfriend? Totally at his mercy to however he wanted to use me. It wasn't being at his mercy that was worrying me, exactly. That was sounding even more fun with the cold weight of the handcuffs in my hand as I walked up the stairs.

What I was most worried about is that he'd satisfy himself and leave me frustrated and horny. I probably deserved it after blowing up at him outside, but I certainly didn't want that outcome.

Evan stood in the middle of the room, his face a thundercloud of energy. Whatever happened next would be a unique, powerful experience for sure.

"What took you so long?" Evan demanded with a scowl.

"I had trouble finding them—"

"Whatever. Are you really ready for this?" Evan asked, holding out his hand for the handcuffs, but not taking a step toward me.

Standing in my doorway, I nodded. My body buzzed with a mix of fear and excitement. "Yes, Evan. I'm always ready for you, though. I wanted you so badly at the club. I wanted you at Will's shop. I want you now more than ever." I was stalling for time while trying to figure out how to ask a question, worrying that asking it would ruin whatever magic was happening between us. "Should we...well, I mean, can—"

Evan's eyes hardened. "Spit it out, James. Don't waste my time."

I blushed at being chastised so firmly, but my dick twitched in anticipation. The mix of emotions confused me, but his command spurred me on. "Safe word. We should have one, right?"

"Right," Evan said. A smile finally appeared. "I almost forgot in my excitement. Good job. What's it going to be?"

I glowed at the compliment while frantically searching for an appropriate word. My mind flashed to us dancing at the club a few days earlier. "YMCA."

Evan smirked, but managed not to laugh at me. "Fine. Now get undressed and get into position."

"Oh. Yes. Good plan." I'd expected to make out for a little bit to get in the mood, not that I needed any help getting there.

I briefly wondered if I was supposed to strip slowly and sexily or as quickly as possible. Following my own needs, I moved quickly, and Evan could correct me if I was doing it wrong.

Just thinking of being corrected felt naughty, but it didn't stop me from getting my boxer-briefs wet and sticky while I wrestled with my belt.

I felt Evan's eyes roving over my skin with each newly exposed area. When I looked up while sliding out of my underwear, Evan's mouth was half-opened. His erection had made a pleasing tent in his pants. It was so unfair that he hadn't started undressing yet, but certainly that phase of our dance would happen...just not soon enough.

Petting my cock, I asked, "Good?"

He shook his head. "You're not in position."

When I didn't move right away, he started counting down from ten. I had no interest in finding out what that punishment would entail, so I scrambled onto the bed, but didn't know which way I should be facing.

"Up or down?" I asked quickly.

He barely stopped counting for long enough to say, "Ass up."

My skin went cold at how vulnerable I'd be handcuffed in that position, but there was no going back now. I *had* to find out how this played out. My curiosity and desire had never been higher.

Fumbling with the handcuffs, I snapped one end around my left wrist, and looped the other around the back of one of the headboard posts. The other end dropped down between the wall and the bed, causing me to lose a couple of precious seconds to pull it back up.

I heard Evan say, "One, zero," just a second before I finally snapped the other end in place. "Ready," I said, smiling as I looked over my shoulder.

"You were late," Evan said, bluntly.

There was no denying it.

Not wanting to wimp out and beg for forgiveness, I instead said, "I guess I need a correction, then, don't I?"

My body tingled again at the powerful word.

Evan nodded, causing me to whimper in nervousness and excitement.

I'd never done anything like it before, either on the giving or receiving end. In fact, my life had been in a rut.

Other than hooking up with Evan, I don't do nearly enough new things. Maybe I'm getting old.

Evan grabbed the lube and a condom from the bedside table. He still hadn't taken off a single piece of clothing. Calm and in charge, he set the items on the bed and climbed on behind him.

Once again, I smiled at him over my shoulder, hoping for him to return the favor.

My body relaxed when he grinned back, but tensed immediately when he said, "Just one more thing," and tied my T-shirt over my eyes.

Robbed of sight, my nerves practically screamed when Evan traced a fingernail in a painfully slow zigzag down my spine. When his hand reached my ass, he gave it a firm squeeze and an even firmer pinch.

"Ouch," I shouted with a yip.

"Is that too much for you, James?" he asked.

His mouth was just above the small of my back. With no other way of tracking him other than his voice and his touch, the hair on the back of my neck stood up as I braced for what would be coming next.

I almost jumped out of the bed when he squeezed my cock and rubbed the tip with his thumb.

"Such a pretty cock." He lightly slapped it and then he was gone.

With him silent and not touching me, I had no idea what was going to happen next. It felt like an eternity. Every inch of my body tried to feel for his presence.

And suddenly his hand exploded against my ass. My head bumped against the headboard. I stifled a giggle for a couple seconds. After that, pain spread over my skin, uncomfortably warm.

I only had a few seconds to wonder if he'd left a handprint on my ass before Evan confirmed it. "Pink looks good on you. I think you need some more."

If he'd given me time, I would have begged for more. I wanted to see how much I could take, and how it would feel afterward. I wanted to make Evan happy.

Plus, I was having fun.

Evan's hand rained down on my ass over and over. The only sounds in the room were the smack of his hand on my skin, and the grunts from me absorbing the pleasurable sting.

Just as quickly as they started, they stopped after a dozen.

"God, James. Your ass is glowing like a Christmas tree. That's wild. How are you doing?"

His hand gently rubbed my skin that was on fire. Even the light touch was almost too much to bear.

"I'm going great." Deciding to embrace to the role, I added a hasty, "Sir."

Somewhere behind me, Evan flipped open the cap on the bottle of lube again, which seemed odd since he certainly hadn't had a chance to undress yet. He also didn't move from where he was kneeling beside my hip.

Something insistently pushed against my asshole and started thrusting without even waiting for me to catch my breath. It took me a second to realize it was Evan's finger.

I breathed out and braced myself with my elbows, once again wishing I could turn and see. But the increased sensitivity from being blindfolded certainly had its own perks, too. I groaned when he added a second finger, and then whimpered when his free hand grabbed my dick and started jacking me off.

The pace escalated so quickly that it was all I could do to keep from falling flat on my stomach.

"I'm going to count down from ten. And then I'm going to stop. If you don't come by then, you'll miss your chance tonight. Ten, nine..."

I only vaguely continued listening to Evan's very slow counting. At least he was giving me a fair chance. With such a tight deadline, I focused on the stretch from his fingers, and the pressure against my prostate. Fireworks were exploding across my body, but the orgasm eluded me.

His hands sped, driving me to heavy panting between gasps of yelling, "Fuck!"

"Three, two..." Evan kissed my tender butt cheek.

I'm not going to make it. I'm so close, but I'm not going to make it.

"Come for me, James."

His magic words unlocked me. I exploded with such ferocity that the silly part of my mind wondered if I'd dehydrate. Evan continued to milk a second wave out of me and didn't stop until he'd forced out the last drop.

I was soaring with euphoria. All sex before had only been going through the motions compared to what Evan had done to me with just his fingers.

Exhausted, I wanted to collapse and sleep, but I'd need Evan to free me from the handcuffs if I planned to avoid falling onto a puddle of my own cum. I was just about to ask Evan to help me out when I realized he wasn't on the bed anymore.

Then I heard the sound of his pants unzipping that forewarned that he was coming back for more. There was no way I'd be able to handle getting fucked after what he'd already done to me. Every muscle in my body was already spent.

I tugged futilely on the handcuffs. The only options were to use my safe word or brace myself to take a rough fucking from Evan.

Which sounds pretty awesome and definitely not the same old rut.

Knowing there'd be plenty of time for sleep when we'd finished, I managed to wiggle my ass to make sure he knew I was ready and willing.

"Good boy," he purred while grabbing my hips.

If I'd thought his fingers had stretched me, his dick taught me the extent of that lie. It took many moments where all I could hear was the pounding of my heart and Evan's frustrated grunts before he finally was fully inside me.

I'm his and he's mine.

"I love you." I barely recognized the words from my own mouth.

Evan froze.

No. Why did I say that? I should have waited for a stunning sunset or holding hands during a cross-country trip or something like that.

The first "I love you" shouldn't be while being speared by his incredible cock.

I was ready to apologize or tell him I was just messing around. Anything to get Evan to get back to fucking me and forget what I'd said. Losing him would devastate me.

He finally moved again, rubbing my lower back, clearly wrestling with how he wanted to reply. I stayed silent to give him whatever space he needed, and just hoped for the best.

"I love you, too, James."

My heart soared. I'd opened myself up to him, and he'd met me halfway.

"We'll talk about that more later," he added and started fucking me as if he were being chased by death itself.

Our bodies slapped together. Our screams bounced around the room.

He was inside me, filling me with more than just his dick. And as magnificent as he was at fucking, the thought of us together, hell, in love even, was bigger and more amazing.

The thought flashed through my mind that I didn't even really know what it meant to be in love.

Will we have to move in together? Share body sponges? Buy groceries together?

I didn't know and didn't care.

Whatever the world decided to toss at us going forward, it would have to deal with us both.

With a final grunt, Evan came, pulling his body hard against mine, where I hoped he'd stay forever. After a few minutes, though, he pulled out, tossed the condom in the garbage can, unlocked the handcuffs and collapsed next to me.

We kissed for several minutes, telling each other that we loved each other repeatedly, eventually using silly voices and giggling until we settled into me spooning his back, holding hands, and my top leg pressed between his legs.

I woke with a start some time well before the sun rose and gave Evan a light squeeze. I whispered, "I wish I'd known it was your birthday. I would have bought you a present."

"Thanks, James," Evan whispered back. "That's very sweet. But you're the only present I need."

"What are you doing awake?" I asked.

"Man, you're hotter than a furnace," he said without moving.

Reluctantly, I rolled off him. "Sorry, you should have said something."

"It felt too good. But thanks. Let's get some shuteye, love. Oh, you'll have to drive tomorrow. My tires got slashed while I was working."

"Mhmm," I mumbled. Evan's words seemed like they should be important, but I was already drifting back to sleep.

21

EVAN

*T*he house was silent when I woke the next morning. I squinted at the bright sunlight that infiltrated the bedroom. The other side of the bed was empty, but since it was James' house, he couldn't have gotten too far away.

Maybe I can talk him into morning sex.

The thought inspired me to get my exhausted muscles moving.

I wasn't sure what I expected to find James doing, probably pushups or cleaning his weapon. But nothing we'd done together prepared me for the shocking site of James lying in his recliner, legs draped over the armrest with a book resting on a pillow on his lap.

And reading glasses.

My knees weakened at the sexy scene while I tried to remember the last time I'd read a book and wondered if assigned reading in school counted. For some reason, instead of telling him how hot he looked, the words that came out of my mouth were, "Hey, nerd."

Without looking up, he replied, "Morning, pipsqueak."

"Did you just call me pipsqueak? That's a deal breaker." I said, flopping onto the couch.

Marking his spot in the book with his thumb, James looked at me over the top of his glasses and very seriously said, "Sorry. I didn't know you were sensitive about your height. You have a swagger that just fits you so well. Compact and edgy just like I like you."

"What? No, man. It's not that. It's that word. 'Pipsqueak.' Who says that, nerd?"

He tsked at me, pushed his glasses up higher on his nose and returned to his book.

"That a good one?" I knew I should let him read in silence. He didn't need to entertain me all day. I'd gotten along just fine before we'd met.

"Yeah. Just some dime-store Western. But they have the best escapes. I finished a Rushdie book the other day, and I love the heavy themes, but sometimes it's nice to just have a good little shootout at high noon, you know?"

I shook my head. "I suppose. I don't read much. I was always more into music. But dime-store Western? Really? Did you go to school with my grandpa?"

"Whatever. Hey, give me like twenty minutes to finish this book and then I'll be yours for the day, okay?" He didn't bother waiting for a reply before turning his attention back to his book.

That must be some shootout.

For some reason, I remembered my mom's text from the night before. I typed a quick text.

Can't come. Something came up. Hot date.

Knowing that Mom hardly ever seemed to remember that she even had a phone, I put my own phone to one side and looked around the room. Since we'd met, I'd been inside his house enough times that I could find the bathrooms, but not enough to remember what kind of print was on the wallpaper border.

Cowboys riding horses. Of course.

I coughed to hide the laugh that threatened to bubble to the surface.

There were two posters on the wall, too. One showed the Atlanta Falcons football team from a high overhead aerial shot. The other showed some race car having its tires changed by the pit crew.

If this works out and we do end up living together, decorating will be...interesting.

My phone buzzed, announcing that my mom had found her phone in record time. Afraid to look, but lacking the resolve to ignore her reply, I picked up my phone.

Raincheck!!! But that's great, honey. What's her name?

She would pick that wound until the day she died, and it would hurt as badly each and every fucking time.

James. You'd like him. He's into horses.

I would have given a hundred dollars to watch Mom's face fall as she read the words. She'd only be happy for me if I was married to a good country girl and we were preparing to pop out children so I could be as miserable as her and Dad.

Oh. You're still doing that. I keep hoping you'll come back to your senses.

For a brief second, I wished James were black, communist, and atheist. Mom would never recover from that.

Closing my eyes, I screamed in my head.

There's no point in ruining a great day just because my mom's still a bitch. It's not like that's any big surprise.

Anyway. Not coming home. Busy now. Bye.

I silenced my phone to make it easier to ignore any replies. To perk myself up, I settled back in on the couch so I could better watch James read. It quickly did the trick, but my stomach growled, begging for some food.

Reluctantly, I stood and stretched. "I'm going to rustle up some food and coffee, cowboy. Want anything?"

"Coffee'd be great. Thanks. Coffee is up—"

"I'll find it." I kissed his forehead. "It'll give me a chance to dig through the cabinets and see what kind of weird shit you're hiding."

He pulled me down for a longer kiss that made toes curl. "If the skeleton pounces, tell him that I'm out and proud now, and he can go fuck off, okay?"

"You are a strange man, James. Perfectly strange."

He'd already returned to his book and probably didn't hear me. Since it looked like he just had a few pages left, I decided to forgive him, and headed to the kitchen.

After getting the coffee brewing and some bread toasting, I found the coffee mugs in the cabinet by the fridge. He had six matching mugs, each a different color. It was like a little gay-pride rainbow caffeine delivery system.

They were all lined up perfectly down to their handles all facing the same direction. It was all so very domestic. One part of my brain knew that I was just picking a fight with myself, but the other side panicked and asked what the hell I thought I was doing settling down.

You need to stay nimble and ready to fly when this all turns to shit, because you know that's how this will end.

That was the real reason that I always pushed men away. I feared the rejection because I believed I wasn't good enough for anything else. It was the one thing that my parents had taught me.

I glanced at the back door.

I can be gone before James ever notices. Safe in my house...next door.

I'll have to move—

When James shouted my name from the other room, I flinched and bumped my funny bone against the counter sending pins and needles down to my fingers.

"Yeah?" I asked, using my good hand to pull down the mugs one at a time.

"This guy in the book named his horse Smoky Bitch. That should be your DJ name. I mean, you smoke and...well, the bitch is just funny."

Laughing much too loudly than the situation called for, I knew everything would be okay. James wasn't sitting around looking for a chip in my armor so he could point at the flaw and use it as an excuse to leave me. He was...just James. Simple, uncomplicated, and perfect.

I poured two cups of coffee while saying, "After how I rode you last night, you're the one that needs to be nicknamed after a horse. Giddy-up."

"Ha ha, now shut up and let me finish this book, Smoky."

My lips almost hurt from how wide I was smiling.

Everything is going to be fine.

"Your coffee is ready whenever you're done," I called through the house. Even that act felt very homey.

James' cellphone rang in the other room. He answered on the second ring.

I found butter and jam in the fridge to add to my toast and was just sitting down to eat when James walked to the kitchen, stopping at the doorway. He leaned forward, grabbing the doorframe with his hands to hold himself up, pleasantly stretching his already-broad chest.

"Hey, bad news," he said. Before my panic could flare up again, he added, "Work called. I have to stop in for some meeting. Really weird. They never call us in for something like that. Wouldn't even tell me what's up. Strange."

"That's fine," I said. "I could use some time to do some chores and run some errands before our hot date tonight. Besides if we hang out all day, I'll run out of things to talk about over dinner."

I'd have to walk, I realized. The damage to the tires felt like so long ago and it wasn't anything I wanted to deal with. I couldn't afford new tires anyway and I wasn't about to let James pay to fix my car again.

"Perfect." He kissed me right after I took a bite of toast. "Mmm. Strawberry. My favorite. I'm going to go shower. Feel free to stay or leave after you eat or whatever, okay. I have some errands around town that I need to deal with sometime today, so I'll take care of them before I stop at the station. Let's plan on meeting back here before dinner."

As I heard him bound up the stairs, I wondered what I'd do to kill the day. Without work or James, I barely knew what to do with myself anymore. I started Snapchatting friends to see what everyone was doing as I finished my toast, hoping someone would be available to keep me company.

22

JAMES

*M*y good mood soured as soon as I walked into the police station and a wave of silence spread around me. Everyone turned to stare, giving me the opportunity to feel what suspects must feel when they got dragged in for questioning.

The only time cops get quiet around another cop is when that cop is in trouble for something. That explained why I'd been called in on a day off, but it didn't answer the other question I had.

What do they think I did?

O'Brian gave me a head nod as I approached his desk, but quickly went back to filling out some paperwork rather than making eye contact.

"Any news on the situation down on The Strip?" I asked, sitting on the edge of his desk and watching Rick and a few other cops whispering to each other at the coffee pot across the room.

"Nope," he said without even looking up from the form.

My work-family had turned on me. It must have felt pretty similar for Evan when he came out to his parents.

It's too bad he won't take me there for his birthday. I'd give them a piece of my mind.

"Maybe you should go wait for the chief," O'Brian suggested.

"So it's going to be like that." I asked, knocking my knuckles on his desk.

"Sorry," he whispered.

There was no way to maintain any amount of dignity while walking to our office's little piece of the Siberian wasteland: the chair outside the chief's office to await punishment.

The only thing cops hated more than criminals was cops who turned bad. Bad cops were the infection that could make the entire police force die unless it was dealt with and chopped off.

Now, I was waiting for the ax.

I'd never been good at waiting. After watching the clock on the far wall announce that five minutes had passed, my foot started tapping rapidly on the floor. My phone provided no distractions since my brain refused to focus on reading any of the words. By the time I pulled my keys from my pack, stuck my finger through the circle on the keychain, and started spinning them, I noticed that I was fidgeting as badly as Evan always did.

He must be rubbing off on me. Man, him rubbing off on me sounds like a much better way to spend the afternoon.

Realizing that Evan would be the perfect distraction, I sent him a text.

Entertain me. I'm going crazy here and think I might be in some kind of trouble.

Typing the words made it more real. There was almost certainly a punishment heading my way, and not the fun kind like getting spanked by Evan before he fucked me last night.

When I started tossing my keys in the air and catching them, Cindy cleared her throat pointedly at me. I didn't stop, though. It wasn't like I'd end up in more trouble because of my fidgeting.

The keys fell to the floor when the front door crashed open.

Marco and Dennis dragged a kicking and screaming Trey into the police station.

"Get your fat, ugly hands off me, pussies. I didn't do a damn thing." Trey shouted.

He was dressed in a sheer, baby-blue shirt, tight white jeans, and those crazy pink combat boots.

He was exactly the man I needed to talk to. He *had* to know something. Five minutes in one of the interrogation rooms, and I'd get to the bottom of it. The rules wouldn't allow it without reason, of course, but it was nice to pretend that I could just bully him into leaking information like they do in the movies.

Watching the cops struggling to hold onto Trey was amusing. They should have just cuffed him if they had a valid enough reason to force him to come to the station in the first place.

Weird.

The cops had dragged Trey most of the way through the station, but Trey hadn't given up on his struggles or his shouting. "I didn't take anything. I didn't touch anything. And I'm not going to say a goddamn thing without a lawyer. Rick, tell these mother-fuckers to let me go."

I did a double-take at the words. Rick didn't look up from pouring creamer into his coffee cup, but Trey wasn't asking Rick for help because they were poker buddies. There was something going on between them.

"Relax, Trey," Dennis said. "We just want to—"

Trey broke free of their grasp and charged for the front door. I was close enough to stop him from leaving. Without worrying about the consequences, or even what Trey had done this time, I sprung from my seat and launched myself into his path. At the last second, I lowered my shoulder into his, and wrapped my arms around his chest.

The crash as we fell against a wall of file cabinets awoke the other stunned officers.

Trey tried punching me, but couldn't get a good enough angle to get any force behind it. He reached toward his pants, figuring he might have a gun tucked in his waistband, I slapped at his hands.

Trey screamed loudly and in a high-pitched voice. "What the fuck, fag? Grabbing my dick the first chance you get?"

Rick, O'Brian, Marco, and Dennis swarmed to my aid.

I was getting ready to tell them to handcuff Trey when the chief shouted, "James. Get in here. Now."

"You guys good?" I asked, checking my hands to see if I'd been cut.

"Yeah, we've got this," O'Brian said. "Nice tackle. Stupid, but good form. You better get in there." He patted my shoulder and nudged me toward the chief.

As I entered the dreaded office to receive my punishment, I looked back at Trey. He had calmed quite a bit. Marco and Dennis were yelling something at O'Brian and Rick. They seemed to come to an agreement.

Marco and Dennis backed off. O'Brian and Rick escorted Trey out of the building.

Why would they do that? Is O'Brian in on it too? That doesn't make sense.

Unfortunately, I didn't get time to ponder the new mystery any further.

The chief barked my name again and sounded more pissed than normal.

The time had come to hear why I was in trouble. Instead of being afraid, though, I was mostly curious.

Things are getting stranger around here by the hour.

23

EVAN

*A*fter quickly growing bored cleaning up my house, I walked downtown, figuring the trip would be safe enough in the daytime. Without anything better to do, I decided to see if Owen had started working yet. If the place was open, I'd mess around with my stage lights again.

I didn't really need them for a place as small as The Firehouse, but it was fun to pretend to be setting up for a bigger venue.

With most of the day to kill before our date, I figured working on the lights would keep me busy and productive. More importantly, it would get me out of the house. Staying cooped up there was somehow more frightening than being out in the city. Hiding at home meant that the problems downtown could reach me in my own living room. I didn't like thinking about that.

Owen was there but the place wasn't officially open that early so it was empty and quiet. He was busy prepping the bar for the weekend rush, and mostly ignored me.

I was on a ladder, fidgeting with the light that was causing the most problems, when I heard a crash of metal out in the alley. I just barely managed to keep my balance and stay on the ladder.

Feeling vulnerable up on the ladder in clear sight of the back door, I hopped down and sought refuge underneath my DJ booth. It didn't take long to realize that I would have been better out in the open of the dance floor. At least I could have run. Trapped in the DJ booth meant that if someone found me, there was nowhere to go.

I wish James was here. He'd know what to do.

I crawled out from under the table and was making my way to the front door when the back door banged open.

"This place makes a lot of goddamn trash," Owen called out to me as he walked back into the bar.

I breathed out a sigh of relief. It wasn't an intruder. Owen had just been taking out the trash. Feeling stupid and embarrassed, but not wanting Owen to know that he had startled me, I stood and stretched before making my way back to my perch on the ladder.

Owen had seen me though. After a quick laugh, he said, "Sorry. I should've knocked." The twinkle in his eye told me that he was not sorry at all.

"Whatever," I said, trying to shrug it off.

"Don't feel bad. I've been a little jumpy when I'm here alone, too. Especially recently with all the things going on. What are you doing up there anyway? Shouldn't you be with James?"

I shrugged. "Mostly just fucking around. I have a few hours to kill and you've been complaining about the lights, so I figured I'd kill two birds with one stone."

Owen nodded as he walked across the dance floor to inspect my work. "The light used to point about here, so these people will be fine now." He took a few steps to the left. "But now these people will get blinded. You need to switch to those laser lights and just shoot them over everyone's heads. Now that would be something to see."

I angled the light down a few inches before realizing that it didn't matter. Anywhere the light would be visible, it would cause problems for someone. Leaving it where it was, I climbed down and started putting the ladder back in the storage room. "I'd love to be able to afford laser lights, but I just don't have the budget. I got these old things for free from the college when they upgraded after the end of the last semester." I said.

"Maybe if you stopped smoking —"

I groaned. "Not you, too? I have to have one vice, okay?"

While walking back to the bar, Owen said, "Maybe you should get into puzzles or origami or something that won't destroy your lungs and kill you while you're still young enough for it to make a difference."

"Yeah, yeah," I sat down across from him at the bar. "Thanks, Dad. I think you need to worry less about my vices and more about getting yourself laid. I bet you won't need to micromanage my life once you find some dick."

Owen pretended not to hear me and continued washing glasses.

"Seriously, Owen. You should just ask out Sean. You guys are already best friends. Why not take it to the next level?"

While stacking the clean glasses, Owen said, "Sean's great, but he's not my type. I'm not his either. That's why we're just friends."

"But why not get some benefits if neither of you are seeing anyone else?" I asked.

"It would just be weird. Once one of us did find someone, how would we stay friends after that? I don't want to ruin the friendship. Besides I've got my eye on someone. Someone more wild and raw or, fuck it. I don't wanna talk about this." Owen dipped his fingers in the water and flicked the drops at me. "But he drives me wild," he added.

I thought he was lying about not wanting to talk about it, so while thinking of James and tracing heart shapes on the bar, I asked, "So when are you going to nut up and ask him out?"

"Soon. I think. I'm just waiting for some kind of sign." Owen set his elbows on the bar and rested his head on his chin. "But enough about me. Besides," he continued. "It's hard to think about dating another guy with these beatings and killings going on. Not all of us have police protection." He waggled his eyebrows suggestively at me, fishing for information. When he saw I wasn't about to start blabbing, he asked, "They catch anybody yet?"

I shook my head. "Not that I've heard of, but I'm just the boyfriend, you know? Who knows what the cops might know or be doing that I haven't heard about. I'm sure they'll catch them soon. It's what they do. James got called in on his day off earlier. Maybe they found out something."

Owen stretched and playfully snapped his towel at me. "I sure hope so. Speaking of James, how are you two doing?"

I rolled my eyes, but it would be futile to *not* give him some information. He'd keep pestering until he was satisfied.

"Great," I said. "Better than I could've imagined. There's only one problem..." I dramatically let myself trail off until Owen looked ready to burst. Then, I added, "We have too much sex. It's like the Nature Channel over our houses. Constant fucking."

"Damn," he said. "You lucky son of a bitch. If he has a friend, you better let me know."

"Like I said, there's only one little problem," I said. "I'm not gonna discount how great the sex is. I mean it really is amazing. Like I can barely walk the next day, but..." I trailed off.

He flipped his middle finger at me. "Enough bragging, man. What's the problem?"

With a sigh, I continued. "Well, with all the sex—did I mention that it was great—we haven't even gone out for a real date yet. But don't worry. We've got plans tonight to go out for my birthday. So we'll see how that goes." I couldn't help teasing him a little more. "But the sex is so great, we'll find a way to make it work out."

"You're killing me, man. Congrats to both of you. The times I've seen you two together, you look happy. It's a good look on you."

Owen grabbed another bag of garbage and hauled it out through the back door.

I went back to messing with the lights for a while. Owen's words about how happy I looked echoed through my mind.

I really do *have it great with James.*

When Owen returned a couple minutes later, we ignored each other for a couple of hours, both busy with our own work. In the end, I said, "They're not right, but they'll have to do."

Owen shrugged. "Get out of here and get ready for your hot date. And happy birthday."

The sun felt great on my face as I walked back toward my house. I stopped at a coffee shop along the way for some caffeine, but didn't linger because I wanted to make sure I was home when James returned. Giddy and excited for the upcoming date, I whistled and wondered what I'd wear.

24

JAMES

*W*hile walking into Chief Paulson's office, I noticed that my nose was bleeding and swore I'd get back at Trey someday before reminding myself that I'm a cop and can't issue vigilante justice.

Chief Paulson stood with his back to me, looking out the window on the far side of his office. Without turning, he said in an eerie monotone, "Well, that little display will make the rest of this easier."

My blood chilled. Our chief wasn't the cheeriest of sorts, but he was a good guy who cared for us cops and always had our backs. Whatever was going on, I was clearly in more trouble than I'd expected.

But what can I even be in trouble for? He can't be mad at me for tackling Trey. That happened after he'd called me.

On my drive over, I'd convinced myself that the chief just wanted to pick my brain to see if I knew anything relevant to the cases. Now it appeared that if I wasn't careful during this meeting, I might be put on desk duty for a while.

How can I protect Evan and all my new friends while sitting behind a desk?

When the chief finally turned to face me, he was holding an envelope. He tossed it onto his desk and said, "Take a look."

My hand shook as I reached for the envelope. "What's this, Chief?"

"Just open the damn thing, James. Don't make this difficult."

I swallowed, but didn't bother delaying any further. Tearing the envelope open, I found a small stack of photos inside. The top one showed me at The Firehouse with Evan. I was leaning in to give him a kiss.

Involuntarily, I smiled at the picture. Under better circumstances, I would have asked Chief Paulson for a copy that I could frame and give to Evan. But whatever trouble I was in stemmed from the picture, and I had no plans to be blacklisted just because I was sleeping with a man.

I wasn't going to back down from it either, though.

"What's the problem?" I asked. "I'm just kissing my boyfriend." It felt liberating to say it out loud at the station. It wasn't any of their damn business and I wasn't going to hide it any further.

"If you look a little more closely, you'll see that you're on duty in the picture," he said.

I looked down and saw my uniform. With a shrug, I said, "Big deal. Every officer here kisses their wife or girlfriend while on duty. You can't tell me it's not okay for me to do the same just because Evan's a man. That's discrimination."

The chief leaned back in his chair. "I don't give a fuck who you sleep with. You're not in here because you're gay. You're in here because you were drinking while on the clock."

My eyes snapped back to the photo. I hadn't noticed the wine glass in my hand. "That's not mine, sir." I decided that politeness was my only chance of getting out of whatever mess I was in now. "One of the guys at the bar, Trey in fact, that guy that caused a commotion out there a minute ago, he handed me his drink to hold for him that night. I didn't drink a drop, sir. I don't drink on duty. You know that."

Chief Paulson looked sad as he said, "Son, I've heard some rumors that you've been drinking too much. This photo certainly isn't helping your case. Right now I think it would be best for everyone if you took a week off, cleared your head, and we'll figure things out when you get back. If you need help, I'll be first in line to make sure you get it."

"This is bullshit, sir. No offense, but you're smarter than that. Half the guys in the station drink too much. It's practically a requirement for advancement, I swear. But this is a set-up. I wasn't drinking. Where'd you get this photo from anyway?"

The chief took the pictures from me and slid them into his desk drawer. "Effective immediately, you're on a one-week suspension. I recommend that you get in touch with your union rep. Don't argue with me about this or it will turn into something longer. Maybe even an early retirement without benefits if you're going to be stubborn. Try to enjoy the week and recenter yourself. I'm not calling you a bad man at all. Just go home and spend some time with your boyfriend and hurry back when the suspension is up. We *do* need you back, you know? But for now go see Cindy to fill out the forms and we'll see you back here in a week. Okay?"

Knowing that arguing would be pointless, I nodded. I tried to look at the silver lining. At least with the free time, I'd be able to spend more time with Evan. With the things going on around the city, it would make me feel better to know that he wasn't out there alone while the danger was still out there.

Shit. His tires.

I'd forgotten the words he'd mumbled the night before. I'd been too tired to pay attention.

If he's not at home, he's walking around alone.

I marched out of the office without another word.

Cindy could barely make eye contact when I approached her

desk. She silently mouthed, "I'm sorry," while handing me a stack of papers. I skimmed them, but couldn't focus on the words. Grabbing the pen she offered, I signed on all the required lines and handed the forms back to her.

"I need your badge and gun," she said.

I pulled my gun from my holster and my badge from my pocket and set them on the counter.

Still whispering, she said, "Keep your nose clean and get back here as soon as possible, okay? Call me if I can help with anything."

I wanted to scream, but knew none of this was her fault. She was just the messenger. Instead I nodded, and said, "Don't let these dumbasses forget that real people are really dying because they can't figure out what's going on."

It felt wrong down to my core to call my fellow police officers *they*, but I wasn't the one who'd suspended me.

Cindy's eyes glanced at a group of cops still hovering around the coffee machine.

Rick was leaning against the wall, grinning like a Cheshire cat.

Leaning down close to Cindy and matching her whisper, I asked, "Is Rick involved with any of this?"

Cindy's eyes shot open wide. "No. Absolutely not. I definitely didn't say anything like that. You should go home now."

"What if I don't believe you?"

She shook her head at me while turning her chair away from me. "Go home, James," she said, no longer whispering.

Knowing I only had a couple of seconds before the other cops came and threw me out of the station or locked me up, I apologized. It was unfair to ask Cindy to risk her own career even if she did know something.

Rick smiled again when his eyes flashed at me while he joked with the other cops. If he knew something, I'd beat it out of him if necessary. I'd force him to admit his involvement in framing me, and then force the chief to rescind my suspension.

I'd only taken a couple of steps toward Rick when the chief stepped out of his office, and practically growled. "Go home. Or you can spend the night in a cell, if you'd prefer."

I wasn't about to throw away my career because of something that Rick had done. He'd never let me hear the end of it. Instead I marched out of the station, throwing the doors wide open as I passed through them.

A few blocks later, I realized I'd left my truck at the station.

I would have left it if Evan's car was drivable. As I returned and walked back through the parking lot, I passed a few other police officers. They all lowered their eyes and refused to say hello. Which was fine. I wasn't in the mood to talk to any of them either. Turning on the radio full blast to try and drown out my own thoughts, I put the truck in gear and pulled out onto the street.

I needed to talk to Evan. He'd find some way to calm me down.

25

EVAN

I nearly fell out of my chair when James burst in through the front door.

"Jesus Christ!" I shouted. "I'm jumping at every fucking shadow these days."

"Sorry. I should have rung the doorbell," James said, looking back at the door door.

"It's okay." I rushed to give him a hug. "You're welcome anytime."

"Thanks. But I know what you mean about jumping at shadows. The cops have got to catch this bastard and get him off the streets. I'm sure we're not the only ones feeling jumpy these days."

Any thought of how weird it sounded to talk about the cops as if he wasn't one flitted away when he squeezed me tightly against his body. I leaned my head against his chest and listened to his heartbeat. His strong body made me feel safe.

"That's an understatement," I said. "I bet half the people that go to The Firehouse are sleeping with their lights on these days. If they're even sleeping at all."

James tipped my head back so he could kiss me. With his lips pressed against mine it was easy to forget about what was happening across the city.

When I remembered exactly why the two of us had spent the morning apart, I pulled away from his lips and asked, "So how was the meeting? They sending you undercover? Top-secret badass mission?"

James let me go and stomped through the kitchen, looking like a violent storm rolling through my house. He yanked open the fridge door, looked around inside, and slammed it shut again.

"Shit. You don't have any beer."

"Yeah," I said. I hated talking about not drinking. Everyone always thought it was weird. I made plenty of bad decisions sober. Being drunk only made that worse. It needed to come up eventually, though. "I don't drink. We can toss some of yours in my fridge, though. It's really no problem. It's not like I'm an addict and can't have them around."

James shook his head. "I should cut back anyway. I probably drink too much. It's just gonna make me fat."

I patted his firm, flat stomach. "I'll still love you when you're my fat cop. We should take plenty of pictures of you with your current hot body, though."

"Anyway," James said, ignoring my banter. He pulled away and sat down at the kitchen table. "The chief suspended me."

I gasped, and wanted to demand answers, but stayed silent since it looked like he had more to say.

"Someone took a picture of me the other night at the club when I was in my uniform and holding Trey's wine glass. Drinking on duty isn't allowed, and apparently I'm getting a repu-tation around the office for drinking too much anyway. I just wish I knew who set me up."

"What shitty timing." My eyes went wide and I quickly added, "Do you think it could have anything to do with the killings? Maybe whoever is doing it doesn't like having a cop sniffing around at The Firehouse all the time? Especially one who lingers there for personal reasons."

James shrugged. "Who knows? It's all bullshit. But at least we'll have more time to spend together. I'll do my week, and then I'll be back on duty and this will soon be a distant memory."

"So I guess you didn't hear any new developments while you were down there, huh?" I asked joining him at the table.

He shook his head. His fingers were rapidly tapping the top of the table.

"Nothing official," he said. "Cindy, our dispatcher, seems to think Rick might be involved, I think. I don't know. Fuck. But she couldn't say anything with him in the room and me in the doghouse. But I haven't trusted Rick since long before any of this started. A lot of that's personal because of his past with my sister. I'm certainly not discounting that some police are involved at this point though and if police *are* involved Rick is on the shortlist of my suspects."

I didn't know what to say. My family was bad, but they certainly weren't involved with any criminal activity. Rick wasn't officially family, but still Rick's past with James' sister had to make things stickier for him to deal with at the office.

"Fuck it," James said. "I don't want to talk about any of this right now." He pulled me onto his lap. I playfully pretended to resist until realizing that I was just cheating myself out of more kisses. As we kissed, I felt his dick stirring against the back of my leg.

"Is that a gun in your pocket, Officer?" I asked.

He shook his head. "They took it away until the suspension is over. That's just me. God, you always make me so horny. What do you say we go upstairs and fuck before the date?"

"I don't know about the people you dated in the past, James, but I'm not just your sex toy, you know?"

James' eyes went wide. "Jesus, I'm sorry. I'm a mess today."

I gave him a quick peck on the cheek before saying, "Don't

apologize. I was kind of kidding. I want to go upstairs and fuck, too. But I don't want that to be all we do. Let's get cleaned up and go out for a night on the town like we planned, and then we'll come home and you can fuck me silly. Or I'll fuck you. Or both. We can make it an all-nighter."

James breathed out a sigh of relief. "That, my super sexy boyfriend, sounds like the perfect way to spend the night. How about I go get my stuff and bring it back over here and we'll get ready together? All domestic like. Hey, it's your birthday. We'll definitely need some dessert to celebrate."

"Well, I certainly won't say no to that."

James stole one more toe-curling kiss before dashing out the back door.

I fidgeted around the house waiting for his return. Fortunately, he only made me wait a few minutes before he rang the doorbell and walked back in carrying a pair of black pants and a pretty, red short-sleeved shirt.

"Wow. You're going to look great. I just hope I have something as fancy so I don't look like a slob next to you. Maybe we'll need to go shopping first."

"Let's go see what you've got. I can get something more casual from home if I need to."

We raced upstairs and started digging through my closet.

"Good lord, you have a lot of t-shirts." James said.

"Yeah, occupational hazard. How about this?" I pulled out a pair of khaki pants and a pale green polo shirt. "I used to wear it to church back when I still lived at home. It's the nicest thing I have."

James nodded. "It's perfect. You'll make it look amazing."

It was silly, but James' compliment calmed my worries. He would still be dressed better than me, but he didn't sound like he'd be disappointed with my appearance. What people thought about how I dressed was a sore subject for me because of the grief my parents gave me while growing up. In their opinions, I was always underdressed for everything. Band concerts, church sermons, birthday parties. What I wore was never good enough for my parents.

James was different. He cared about me, not how I dressed and how that would make him look.

I rubbed my hand on his cheek. "Can you shave before we go? I like the stubble, but if we're going to be making out a lot, smooth is the way to go."

"Sure, I'll get my razor."

I grabbed him as he turned to leave. "I've got one. You can borrow mine."

When I dragged him toward the bathroom, he didn't protest.

As we stood next to each other at the sink, shaving and brushing our teeth and getting ready for the night, it all felt so very domestic. I could certainly get used to living my life with a man like James. After years of me pushing everybody else away, I was starting to worry about what would happen if James ever got tired of me.

I begged karma to leave this one alone.

"Hey, if I have to shave, you should too," James said after he finished with his own face.

James dabbed shaving cream on my cheek and rubbed it over my five-o'clock shadow. When I reached for the razor blade, he slapped my hand away. "I'll take care of you."

With one hand on my chin, he dragged the razor against the right side of my face. I had zero worries about being hurt. James would never let anything hurt me.

The simple moment felt so sweet and sensual that my heart was ready to burst.

As soon as he finished with my beard, I lunged forward to give him a kiss.

Laughing, he pushed me away, saying, "At least wash the shaving cream off first."

Instead I grabbed the back of his neck and kissed him all over his face until we were both giggling and messy.

"Damn, Evan. I can't wait until we get back home and can hop into bed."

I glanced at my bed, more than half-tempted to call off the date and get right to the sex, but it seemed like I'd be cheating myself out of something special. "Me either," I said, dragging him into the bedroom and tossing his clothes at him.

A few minutes later we were both dressed and heading out the door for our big first date.

26

JAMES

*W*ith a couple of hours until dinner, and knowing that we'd end up naked, sweaty, and tired if we hung around the house, we decided to drive down to The Strip and take a stroll along the riverwalk instead. Neither one of us had a clue about which flowers were which without reading the placards, but neither of us cared while we lazily walked along the river dividing Augusta, Georgia and North Augusta, South Carolina while holding hands, stealing kisses.

"What are you going to do about work? Is a suspension a big deal?" Evan asked while we watched a bee flitting from flower to flower in one of the gardens.

Evan sat down on a nearby bench, giving me plenty of time to reply. His calmness was a major contrast to the twitchy, bouncy, impulsive man who'd stormed across my yard to yell at me not all that long ago. I loved both sides of his personality, but thought this calmer, more mature man could easily be the one I wanted to spend the rest of my life with.

This is too crazy of a whirlwind. Slow down, cowboy.

Joining him on the bench, we grabbed each other's hands. It

was an automatic move already. I'd never been so quick to hold hands with any of the women I'd dated.

"Yes and no," I finally said. "It depends. I should be fine, though. I've never been in trouble before at work."

"What exactly happened?"

"Remember when Trey handed me his glass so he could run off to pee, or flirt with someone, or whatever?"

Evan shook his head.

"Well," I continued. "Someone in there must have snapped a picture."

"Who?"

It was my turn to shake my head. "No idea. The chief wouldn't tell me."

"Wasn't that cop friend of yours there that night? O'Hara?"

"O'Brian," I corrected, while trying to think back on the details of the night. "Yeah. He chased the guys down the alley."

"Maybe you should talk to him and see if he saw anything." Evan offered.

That was the night O'Brian lost two perps in a closed alley. What if there weren't any guys there and he was the one who took the pictures? But why?

"Yeah, I think I will have to have a talk with him when I see him again."

I couldn't believe that O'Brian was mixed up in any of this, but if he wasn't, and he didn't take the pictures, what had he hoped to gain? Was he trying to make himself look better for a promotion?

I brought Evan's hand to my mouth and gave it a quick kiss. "You know what the shittiest part is? I've cut way back on drinking since we started dating."

Evan hugged against my arm. "That sounds nice. The dating, not the rest," he quickly added.

I tipped my head to rest it on his and looked at the gardens.

The vibrant colors danced with the lengthening shadows as the sun started diving toward the horizon.

"New topic," I said. "What's the endgame with the DJ thing? You seem pretty good, but I won't lie, I don't know shit about it. You going to disappear to Europe to DJ in arenas over there someday?"

"Mmm. What do I want to be when I grow up? The million-dollar question. I've been thinking about that a lot over the last year. Before meeting you, my goal was to find a way to get as far away from my family as possible. Now..."

"Now what?" I pushed, breathlessly.

"Now, I don't care as long as I'm close to you." Evan sat up quickly and added, "Not that I'm trying to rush anything, but, you know?"

"Yeah, man. I know. There's something here, right?" I tapped his chest and then mine. "Something real. It's crazy and I love it. I love you and want to see where this takes us."

Evan sighed.

"What's wrong?" I asked, suddenly worried that I had gone too far.

"I just wish there was an easy way for us to be together here and for me to take a shot at the big career. I should probably lie and say it doesn't mean anything to me." He flashed a quick, nervous smile at me. "But it's important that I'm honest with you. It's going to be something we'll have to work through."

"Noted, and thanks for trusting us to work it out. But don't think that I'm necessarily stuck here in Georgia." The bee, drunk on nectar, flew off over our heads, returning home. "I could be a cop anywhere, after all. Plus, I love protecting people, but I hate the bureaucracy some of the time. I've thought about becoming a PI or even a bodyguard for a hot, new, superstar DJ."

Evan snorted. "Don't be silly." He leaned back against my shoulder.

"What?" I pretended his words hurt me. "I'm not good enough to be your bodyguard?"

"Jesus, you're serious?" He pulled his head out from under mine again. All the up and down reminded me of the twitchy Evan I'd first met. He looked at me with a serious expression on his face, trying to tell if I was pulling his leg. "Of course I'd trust you to be my bodyguard, but that's a lot of eggs to put into one basket. What if the DJ thing doesn't work out? You should go the private investigator route so we have that to fall back on."

"Deal," I said, making sure to keep any hint of a smirk from my face.

"Deal," Evan agreed, holding out a hand to seal the pretend agreement we'd just made.

I grabbed the hand and pulled him closer for a kiss, making sure to close my eyes and enjoy the moment. "There. Now that we've agreed, I'll have to take a couple of business classes at the college to learn how to even get started running my own business."

"Perfect. I'll use the time to put together some original songs and try to line up some gigs outside of The Firehouse."

Everything that we'd been saying hit me at once. We were really committing to each other and making plans like we expected to stay together long-term. Rather than feeling any fear or doubt, though, I wanted to run straight to the college to sign up. A future away from home with Evan was sounding even better than living in Georgia with him. Between the recent crimes and my questionable suspension, a change of environment didn't sound all that bad.

"Damn," I managed to say. "All of this talk is making me hungry. What do you want?"

Evan looked out over the river. "Let's cross the bridge. We'll go to that Hungry Elephant just over in South Carolina and get hot dogs and ice cream in another state. That sounds better than Mexican."

"Sounds perfect. Should be quick and we can get back home for the real dessert."

I pulled Evan to his feet and hurried him toward the bridge.

27

EVAN

We'd already had hot dogs and were moving on to our dessert.

How can such a simple, boring date be so amazing and exciting?

Looking at James with his face nearly pressed against the glass while trying to decide which kind of ice cream to get for his third scoop, the answer was obvious.

Everything is better with James.

"I just can't make up my mind, but toss some birthday cake in there. Fits the occasion." He stood up and gave me a hug.

"Is it your birthday, sir?" the girl working behind the counter asked me.

"Tomorrow," I replied, trying not to blush and wondering why I was doing it in the first place.

"Happy birthday. Ice cream is free for birthday boys. If you don't tell, I won't," she said with a wink.

James fist pumped. "I still get credit for being willing to pay, right?"

I rolled my eyes and shook my head. "Who said you were paying? The ice cream was my idea. My treat and don't you say another word about it."

James sighed and stomped his foot, pretending to be upset, but didn't bother to challenge my statement.

For some reason it was important to me to pay for our meal. James had taken such good care of me so far, even dropping everything to help me with my car. Paying a few dollars for a couple of hot dogs and our ice cream was the least I could do to make myself not feel like a kept man. I hurried to hand my credit card to the girl.

The casual ease with which James shrugged it off and didn't make it a big deal over who paid meant a surprising amount to me. It showed that even together, I'd still have independence.

Or something. I had no idea what I was telling myself. None of it made sense. But James had that effect on me.

When someone cleared their throat behind us, and we turned toward the sound, James squeezed my hand.

The voice belonged to a young man wearing a t-shirt with the college logo on it.

"Hi." His eyes darted around the room.

Worrying that we were about to be pranked or worse, I scanned the restaurant, but we three were the only customers.

With a cheery voice, James said, "Can we help you?"

The guy cleared his throat again. He looked so young and nervous.

How did I manage to move out on my own at that age? Did I look that afraid of everything?

Shivering at the memory of my walk home in the dark the other night, I pushed the thought aside.

That was genuinely creepy. I certainly wasn't afraid in the light of day back then.

"Are...I mean...shit. Are you a cop?" he finally managed to ask James. "You look familiar."

"Yeah. I'm on...vacation right now, but I'm a cop. Can I help you?" James' voice, while still friendly, had dropped into his cop voice. Calm and in control.

Sexy.

"Great. My name's Doug. Well, I was wondering if you knew anything about the attacks on those guys on The Strip. I can't get a straight answer," Doug said.

"Not enough, unfortunately. If you have any leads, we'd love to hear about them. You can call the main office or talk to any of us cops."

"It's that fucking college," Doug said.

James shot me a confused glance. "Excuse me?" he asked.

"The admins will cover up anything to keep it out of the news. I've heard of five students getting beaten bad enough to get sent to the hospital. All around the sports dorms where I live. We're terrified over there, but will the college bring in outside help? No way. Fuckers."

"Sorry. I don't know anything about that." James said, patting Doug on the shoulder.

Poor Doug looked close to tears. He said, "I'd transfer but after this summer I'll just have two semesters left. I guess I'll just keep my head down and stay home after dark."

Doug turned to leave.

"Hey," I said, my gaydar finally pinging. "Are you twenty-one?" When he nodded, I added, "Gay?" He nodded again, looking back over both shoulders. "If you want to get out some night, feel free to come down to The Firehouse on The Strip. It's probably not much safer than anywhere else, but at least we can all band together, right?"

Doug nodded. "Yeah. That sounds great. I've been pretty silent about being gay. It wouldn't really go over that well on the baseball team. But fuck it. Senior year, right?"

Doug finally smiled again before heading out the door.

James squeezed me tightly. "That was a good thing you did."

"Experience, I guess. I've got the tire tracks on my soul to prove it. That's pretty much how I found The Firehouse, you know. Trey took me under his wing pretty much the same way. I guess it's just my turn. I'm a grown-ass man, after all."

James smirked. "Where do you put the hyphen?"

"We'll have to hurry up with our ice cream when it's ready so I can show you."

The silly banter was so effortless with James. I didn't worry about sounding like a dork around him and it felt amazing to just say whatever I was feeling without worrying about being judged or tossed to the curb.

"Speaking of Trey. I really need to talk to him. There's no way he doesn't know something. I need to ask him some questions. Think you can set that up?"

I shrugged. "I'm not sure if he'll be talking to me anymore, but I can give it a shot. I saw him the other day. He was way weird and bizarre. He definitely seems to think that those friends of yours, Rick and O'Brian, are involved in the killings somehow."

"Bullshit," James said, a rare thundercloud during our otherwise fantastic night.

I wasn't in any mood to argue. "Probably. Trey seems pretty messed up, but you shouldn't discount it just because you don't like him. Trey knows the streets better than anyone."

"Sorry. Of course I shouldn't. But Rick and O'Brian? You know what? Fuck it. I'm not on duty tonight. We'll think it all through some other time. Right now, I just want to focus on you."

Just like that, the storm had passed. Still feeling a little edgy, but wanting to help keep the date positive, I stood on my tiptoes and gave him a peck on the lips. I gasped when James lifted me off the ground, but when his lips pressed firmly against my own, I wrapped my legs around his waist and my hands around his neck, and settled in for the more leisurely and passionate kiss that James delivered.

The ice cream girl cleared her voice before calling our names. "Your ice cream is ready, sirs."

As I dropped out of his grasp, James laughed and said, "Sirs? Man, this place is making me feel ancient."

We took our ice cream cones to one of the tables outside.

The shadows from the buildings covered everything as dusk approached.

"What do you want to do next?" I asked. "Dancing? Movie? Home?"

Ice cream dripped down over my fingers. Before I could find a napkin, James pulled my fingers into his mouth and slowly sucked them clean, teasing the fingertips with his tongue.

"Whatever you want, birthday boy," he said.

"I think we should go home. We're dressed completely wrong for the occasion." I said while dipping my finger in my ice cream.

James' eyes stared at my finger while he said, "But I thought you said I looked great earlier."

I nodded and very slowly raised my finger toward my lips. James swooped in at the last second to suck it clean again.

My dick throbbed with need.

The hunger in James' eyes was palpable.

"Oh, you do, James. But it's my birthday party. We should have worn our birthday suits and spent the night blowing out each other's candle."

He snorted, but shifted in his seat. "I would love to see you in that suit. The only thing I'd like to see more is my dick in your birthday suit."

I threw back my head to laugh. "That's horrible, man. I mean, cute, I suppose, but it seems like you crossed into creepy there. You'll have to try harder than that."

"I can't get any harder than I am right now, Evan." He pulled my hand against his dick to prove the point.

"Oh my. We should get you home and take care of that medical condition," I said, giving his thick cock a squeeze.

James gasped. "What do you have in mind, doctor?"

"Well, considering we don't know what's causing this to

happen, we should start with a full body inspection. We'll probably need to do some probing to get to the root of the problem,
but I'll leave no nook unlicked."

James dipped his tongue into his ice cream and immediately
kissed me, his chilled tongue a dramatic contrast to our hot-
blooded desires. It took no time for the ice cream to melt on our
tongues.

"It's your birthday, so whatever you want, but I'm ready to go
home if you are," James said, shifting again in his seat.

"Sure thing," I said. "After I finish my cone." I took a slow lick
around the base of the ice cream and sat back, pretending that I
planned to take a long time finishing.

James growled in frustration, but didn't say anything to
rush me.

With a laugh, I said, "Relax. I can eat while we walk. Let's go."

James sprang to his feet before I'd even finished the words.

28

JAMES

*E*van had really done a number on me with his flirtations at the ice cream shop. Taking the time to slow things down and give ourselves some space to talk had completely ramped up my desire. Evan was so much more than a pretty face and hot body.

But the fact of the matter was he *was* a pretty face and a hot body, too.

As we both raced to my truck, I was glad that the bridge between the two states was so short. Back in Georgia, our excitement about returning to my house helped us hurry through the downtown. We paused at street corners long enough to kiss until the light changed, before dashing off again.

I knew nothing could ruin our perfect night.

I was wrong. So wrong.

Halfway down the block, we saw Trey talking to the guy from the ice cream shop. Trey had regained his familiar swagger and Doug was practically eating out of his hand.

Trey leaned over Doug, looking like a lion about to eat a rabbit. And the rabbit looked ready to die and go to heaven. When Evan said we should stop and say hi, I nodded. It would give me a chance to ask him a couple of questions. But the busy intersection stopped us from crossing the street right away to join them.

As we watched them, Trey said something that made Doug take a step back. Trey reached out to grab his hand and keep him from running away. Doug nodded at whatever bullshit Trey was whispering to him, but he didn't look like he was buying whatever Trey was selling.

Wait. What is he selling?

Some things finally became clear. With Trey's connections and prestige in the gay community, he would be a great drug dealer. He knew all the gay men in the city, and helped many of them out when they were struggling. Most of them would do anything for him.

Something didn't quite make sense, though. If Trey was recruiting college kids to work for him, how was he the one that had ended up beaten in the alley? Was it just a bad drug deal?

I couldn't shake the idea that Rick and O'Brian might actually be involved somehow. Just because I couldn't see the connection right then didn't mean that there wasn't one.

I needed to get some answers out of Trey. Wherever I turned, he seemed to be involved in all the questions that arose. It was easy to believe that Rick was involved, but what was the connection with O'Brian?

It had to be a mistake. O'Brian was too goofy to have gotten himself mixed up in any crimes bigger than parking in a no-parking zone.

Evan darted through the red light when he saw a break in the traffic. I hurried after him.

"Trey, leave Doug alone," Evan yelled, shoving his body into Trey.

Trey made a fist but thought better of it when he looked at me.

"That's right," I growled, stepping between Trey and Evan. "I just want to ask you a couple of questions. You touch anyone and I'll arrest you."

"You're not arresting shit," Trey said with a laugh. "You're not even a rent-a-cop anymore. I saw them kick your ass out of the station this afternoon."

"I just want to ask you some questions." I repeated, trying to look friendly.

When I took a step toward Trey, he backed away. I didn't pursue. He wasn't going to talk anyway. I wasn't looking for a fight, but I didn't want him involving Doug in whatever shit he was shoveling.

Behind me, Evan told Doug, "You should be careful with Trey. He'll use you and toss you aside."

Trey snorted. "Look who's talking. Isn't that your M.O.?"

"Trey, I've done some stupid shit. Those days are behind me. What's your excuse?" Evan said, sounding like twice the man that Trey would ever be. "Why don't you just answer James' questions? You're just as likely to get hurt as anyone. Maybe more so."

Trey didn't answer. He looked up and down the block. Whether he was expecting more trouble or backup, I wasn't sure, but I didn't particularly want to stick around to find out.

"Doug, we'll give you a ride home," Evan said. "Trey isn't the kind of friend you need to be making."

I felt Evan standing close to my side, ready to support me through whatever happened with Trey.

I wished Evan had taken Doug and left me alone with Trey. Trey almost certainly had a gun handy and I would have felt a million times better if Evan were nowhere around while that threat loomed, especially with the way Trey glared at us with all the hate in the world in his eyes.

Talking slowly and quietly to make sure I didn't startle Trey, I said, "Man, I don't know what you're mixed up in, but it's not going to get better until you come clean. And if you're somehow mixed up with the beatings and killings around here...well, more of that is not going to help you at all."

"What the fuck do you know, civilian?" Trey's words cut me deep. He smirked at the damage they caused.

I didn't like losing my badge, especially since I hadn't done anything wrong. It had been Trey's wine, after all.

Shit. What if O'Brian had really been there because of something with Trey rather than the phantoms he'd said he'd been chasing down the alley.

Realizing there was a connection there felt big, but I didn't risk letting it distract me from Trey and the gun I worried he might pull at any minute. "Yeah, about that. You had something to do with me getting suspended, didn't you? Did you take that damn picture? Did you get O'Brian mixed up in this shit?"

"As if O'Brian needed an invitation. I didn't take your picture, cornflake," Trey laughed. "That was all just a fortunate coincidence, but not my doing. If you cops want to take yourselves out, it ain't nothing to me."

O'Brian. But why? How is he involved in this?

Trey backed away as I lunged at him. One way or the other, I was going to make him talk.

Evan tugged at my shirt to stop me. "Trey," he said. "If you know something, you need to talk to the cops. Maybe not James, but someone. Our friends are at risk. Shit, you almost died. This is too big to just bullshit your way through. It isn't a game anymore."

Trey flashed his middle fingers at us and headed back toward the intersection.

I made a decision to not pursue him. My only goal was to get Evan and Doug away from him safely. We'd drop Doug off at his dorm and Evan and I would hurry back to my house to finish his birthday.

No drama.

It wasn't like I had any authority to arrest Trey or force him into some kind of confession. We just needed to get home safely. I'd pass along my suspicions to the Chief in the morning and let them take it from there until they gave my badge back to me.

And then we heard the gunshot.

A few blocks away.

In the direction of The Firehouse.

Instead of doing the smart thing and hurrying to the truck, Evan and I ran toward the club. Doug followed us.

I had no idea where Trey went. That felt like a problem.

29

JAMES

I led Evan down a side street, hoping that all of the action would be on the main street.

When I slowed and Evan and Doug tried to run past me, I pulled them to a halt. Evan's eyes were wide open and darting around wildly.

"What if they killed one of our friends?" he asked. "We've got to get over there and make sure they're okay."

The streets had gone eerily quiet, I pulled out my phone to dial 911. "Let me call this in. We can't just go charging into a gunfight without backup. Doubly so when we don't know what's actually happening."

Before I could hit dial, another gunshot exploded a couple of blocks to our right. Evan jumped away from the sound and bumped into me, causing me to drop my phone which fell to the ground. The screen shattered, the case fell open, and the battery bounced across the sidewalk.

Putting it together was taking too long and Evan had already started walking away. I finally managed to get the battery in place and snapped the case together but the phone wouldn't turn on.

Cursing in frustration, I threw the phone against a nearby

building and jogged to catch up with Evan. When I caught him, I tugged on his sleeve and said, "Slow and steady."

As great as Evan looked in his tight khakis, I wished he'd worn something baggier and not left his phone at home.

My fingers twitched, begging for the comfort of my gun. Even though I rarely pulled it from its holster outside of the range, it was always there ready to help me out in a pinch. Without it and my bulletproof vest, I felt very mortal and small.

I heard Doug's footsteps behind me. Not sure whether he'd be better off staying in a group with us or trying to get home on his own, I ignored making any decisions for him. He was a grownup.

At our cautious pace it took a few minutes to get back near The Firehouse. We were still a block away when the cop cars sped past in a whirlwind of red flashing lights and loud sirens.

The cavalry had arrived just in time. Encouraged by their arrival, I started jogging after them, making sure Evan and Doug stayed close behind. At least we wouldn't be going into trouble alone.

There's no way the whole station is in on whatever's going on with these crimes, I said to comfort myself.

The scene around The Firehouse was pandemonium. A couple hundred people who'd arrived early to start partying had gathered from various nearby clubs in front of The Firehouse. Everyone was milling around in the middle of the street, holding up their cellphones to stream live video of the events on their social media pages, and talking excitedly with their friends.

Cops were busy pushing the crowd back, trying to get them far enough away to keep them safe while other cops were planning their attack.

I'd never been stuck on the civilian side of the police barricade before. Feeling helpless and useless, I blended in with the rest of the crowd and stood behind Evan with Doug at our side. We all watched the cops spreading out and trying to assess the scene.

"Evan. James. Over here." Owen stood a little to our left waving for us to join him. Liam and Sean stood on each side of him. Sean looked like he would have preferred to go home, but the gravity of the crowd kept him in the center of it. Liam looked ready to storm all of the buildings and ferret out any criminals inside.

I hoped he wouldn't do anything stupid. The last thing the police needed was civilians jumping into the fray. It wasn't like the bad guys wore uniforms that made them easy to identify, and when gung-ho regular people tried to play hero it made the cops' job that much more difficult.

"What's going on?" Evan asked.

"I don't know," Owen answered. "We were inside. It seemed like a normal evening until we heard the gunshot. It was close. We're pretty sure it was either in the alley or the strip club behind The Firehouse."

"Hey," I said when I saw Liam creeping toward the front of the crowd. "Everyone needs to remember to stand back. If you're not trained to deal with the situation, you'll just get in the way and get yourself or someone else killed."

Owen reached out and pulled Liam back to him. Liam looked at us all as if surprised to learn that he'd been walking away from the group.

Leave it to the drummer to be the crazy guy to accidentally put himself in the path of the bullets.

The guys all stood around catching up. Evan introduced Doug to everyone. It sounded like Doug was going to fit in just fine.

Good for him.

I heard the topic quickly switch from the shootings to our date. It had only been a few minutes ago, but it already felt like a million years ago.

Not knowing how to make small talk during a crisis, I watched the SWAT team break off into groups and set up around the strip club. They were preparing to storm the front door. I knew this was just the calm before the storm. Once the chief gave the command, they would crash through the front door, toss their flashbangs to confuse the bad guys and start their sweep of the building. The whole routine would take just a few minutes if it went well.

The SWAT team practiced so often that it almost always did.

Something caught the corner of my eye. Turning my attention to the alley I saw Trey disappearing into the shadows. None of the other cops seemed to notice him. Forgetting my suspension and the fact that I didn't have any weapons, I crept toward the alley. I was halfway there before I heard Evan calling out to me to come back.

With the blood pounding in my ears and the taste of copper in my mouth, I couldn't obey. I had to get Trey. Whatever else happened in the strip club next door, I had to make sure Trey was apprehended. He was some part of the very real threat to Evan and me, and I was certain he was mixed up in everything else that was happening, too. Letting him go free simply wasn't an option.

I took two steps into the alley but didn't see any sign of Trey. He'd either escaped into the strip club or The Firehouse, or was hiding in the dumpster.

Realizing exactly how much danger I was exposing myself to, I managed to stop myself from running to check the dumpster.

As I turned to flag down a cop and let him know they needed to keep their eyes open for Trey, two sets of impossibly strong hands grabbed me and dragged me deeper into the alley.

I kicked and tried to scream, but, with one of the hands pressed tightly over my mouth, no one heard me.

When they'd dragged me deeper into the alley, the two men said something to each other that I didn't understand. In my panic, I couldn't even begin to guess at the language.

I tried kicking backward, hoping to catch one of them in the nuts and give myself a fair chance to fight my way free. My kick barely landed on one of their thighs. The man grunted, but did not let me go. Instead his friend threw a punch that landed just below my eye. The first guy pulled me against his body and covered my mouth with his hand.

It smelled like sauerkraut.

"Bite me and I break your neck," he whispered into my ear.

Further into the alley I heard two voices arguing. One belonged to Trey. I recognized the other, too.

O'Brian.

"What the fuck are you doing over here? I thought I told you to go home." O'Brian hissed at Trey.

"Boss," Sauerkraut whispered. "What you want us to do with this guy?"

"I was on my way," Trey said. "I even had a friend who was ready to watch Netflix and chill. Your buddy cockblocked me, though."

"Boohoo for you. That doesn't explain why you're here in this alley, though. With what's going down in the strip club, you shouldn't be anywhere in this fucking state."

"Yeah, well, your buddy knows you're involved and I thought you might want to take care of that loose end before it took care of you. But I can go home and rub one out instead."

"Boss! This guy. Should I ice him?"

O'Brian and Trey both turned their heads and noticed me for the first time.

"Well, look at that, O'Brian," Trey said, flashing a smile. "You white guys really are lucky motherfuckers."

"Damn it, James. You shouldn't be here," O'Brian said under his breath when he noticed me.

"O'Brian, let me go." I struggled uselessly against the two men who were still holding me. "You can't just kill me in the alley with cops running around everywhere."

"Yeah. I know," O'Brian said, more than a small touch of

sadness in his voice. Before I could relax, though, he gave his command to his goons. "Take him into The Firehouse."

Any further struggles were cut short when a third man I hadn't noticed stepped in front of me and punched me in the temple, making the world go black.

30

EVAN

*W*hat the hell is James doing snooping around in the alley?

I flinched at the sound of another shot from inside the strip club and dropped to my knees with my hands over my head. Everyone screamed. At one point I realized that I was screaming, too. Some cops yelled for everyone to go home, but everyone remained frozen exactly where they were.

When I managed to get back to my feet, Sean grabbed ahold of me. Tears streamed down his face. "Is everyone in there going to be okay?" he asked.

Sean needed some kind of encouragement, but it was hard to believe that all of those gunshots had merely been warning shots. Still, it wouldn't do him any good to make him face reality at that moment.

I gave him a hug and said, "The cops know what they're doing, Sean. If we all stay out of their way to let them do their job everything will be fine, I'm sure."

Remembering that James was doing his best to do exactly the opposite of staying out of their way, I shot a glance back toward the alley, but couldn't see any sign of him.

Hoping that he'd decided to go talk to his cop buddies rather than taking on the bad guys single-handedly, I tried to look through the crowd at all the places the cops had gathered into groups, but still didn't find him.

"Owen and Liam, can you see him? James was over by the alley a second ago but now I can't find him. You're tall, find him."

Owen and Liam standing on their tiptoes could easily see over the crowd. Owen turned back to me first. The sadness in his eyes told me all I needed to know, but in case there was any doubt, he added, "I don't see him, Evan."

Liam looked at me with the same sympathy on his face. "I'm sure he's just lost in the crowd. He'll show up. He knows how to handle these situations, right?"

I forced myself to nod, but I knew we were all lying. Something had happened to James. He was in trouble. He needed help but the cops were tied up with their own problems.

Help wouldn't come fast enough.

"Yeah, sure," I lied. "You must be right. I'm going to walk through the crowd a little bit and see if I can find him. Maybe he's looking for us. It's gotta be better than standing here doing nothing. If he shows up, tell him to wait here."

Sean squeezed my hand. "Be careful. Come right back, okay?"

I nodded rather than lying to him directly. Pushing my way through the crowd, hoping beyond hope that I would actually find James, I looked for ways to get through the police barricade. It only took me a minute to realize that I'd attract too much attention if I tried to sneak into the alley, which was blocked by their barricade. It wasn't like the cops would recognize me and ignore me like they had seemed to do with James.

Looking around for another option, I noticed that their barricade stopped short of The Firehouse's entrance. Moving toward the door before I had a chance to change my mind and come to my senses, I thought of all the angry things I would yell at James when I found him.

I wasn't the type of guy to fall for just any old Tom, Dick and Harry, so who did he think he was to risk getting himself killed right after we'd been talking about our future possibilities together?

Who is going to be my bodyguard when I become a big famous DJ if he gets himself killed in that stupid alley?

Moving slowly and trying to make myself as small as possible, I hoped to avoid attracting attention as I moseyed across the sidewalk. My plan involved getting to the alley through the back door of The Firehouse, and if I didn't find James in the alley, I'd just have to rescue his stubborn ass from whatever the hell was going on inside the strip club.

Just as my hand reached the door handle, a voice behind me cut that plan short when he shouted for me to stop.

"You can't go in there. This area is closed off. Step away from the door and get back with the rest of the crowd. Even better, take your friends and go home," the cop said. "Seriously, I don't know what you idiots are thinking hanging around here. It's way too dangerous."

I wondered what he would do if I shrugged and opened the door anyway.

I didn't get the chance to find out, though.

We all jumped at the sound of another gunshot. An instant later the concrete chipped and a little cloud of dust rose up near the cop's feet from where the bullet hit.

A voice called out over his walkie-talkie. "What the hell's going on over there, Rick?"

The cop shouted back into his walkie-talkie. "We have bullets coming out of the building now. Repeat. Live bullets coming out of the building. Send that crowd home and get the SWAT team ready to storm the place, damn it."

While the cop was distracted, I quietly pulled the door open and snuck into The Firehouse.

When the door shut behind me, it blocked off most of the outside sound, leaving the room mostly silent.

What am I doing?

Three men stood with their backs to me on the dance floor, laughing at something on the ground that I couldn't see. One of them kicked the lump and made it grunt in pain. The man to his left took his turn. I felt bad for guy on the ground, but had no idea what I'd be able to do against three men.

Why didn't I demand that the cops storm the alley and save James instead of going off like I'm some kind of superhero?

The kicked man tried to get to his feet, but was sent back to the floor with another kick. But not before I'd been able to see his face.

James.

Without thinking, I ducked down low and crept straight toward them. I had no idea what I would do when I got there, but I had to try something. I couldn't let them kill James. He needed me to do something.

A few feet from the booth, I realized that the smart plan would have been to go back outside and drag an army of cops back in with me. I needed a weapon, but other than my lighter I didn't have anything useful. Other than maybe throwing a chair at them, I didn't have any options for helping James.

The three men would have no more trouble killing the two of us than they would killing just James alone.

I was useless.

I froze when I heard two more voices arguing in the corner. One sounded familiar, but in my panic, I couldn't place it. It seemed so far away and unimportant compared to the men kicking James.

Realizing that sitting there letting time pass was only working against me, I worked up the nerve to do the smart thing; to head back to the front door, hoping to beg the cops for help. I'd only made it two steps when the front door burst open and a cop miraculously burst through the door with his gun held out in front of him. Instead of saving James, though, he aimed the barrel at me and shouted, "Get on the fucking ground."

From across the room, I heard James shout, "Rick! No!"

Managing to put together that Rick was James' nephew's father, the one who James and Trey thought were involved in the crimes, I knew we'd never get out of this alive.

I hated how weak and powerless Rick and his gun made me feel. And for what? So he could sell drugs and hate men who lived differently than him? It wasn't much different than my parents' judgment and refusal to accept me because of their hatred.

Why is there so much hate in the world?

Done cowering to people who thought they were better than me, I decided that if this was to be my last moment, I'd face it bravely rather than cower.

Standing tall, I glared at Rick and shouted. "Whatcha going to do, you fucking dirty cop?"

Rick answered by pulling the trigger.

31

JAMES

*E*van crumpled to the ground like a rag doll, but quickly curled into a ball. He was moving and wasn't screaming. Somehow Rick's bullet had missed him. That might have been the most surprising moment of the night. Rick was the best marksman I knew. He didn't miss on accident.

What game is he playing?

"There you are," I shouted. "I knew you had to be involved in all of this somehow."

Before Rick could answer, someone groaned near me. Risking a glance, I saw one of the dicks who'd been kicking me, lying on the ground, writhing in pain. Rick's bullet had taken him down.

The other two men jumped behind me as if they had something to worry about with Rick and hoped I would be their shield. Knowing that Rick had plenty of bullets to take me and them all out, I wasn't sure their plan had much merit.

Confused, but not one to look a gift horse in its mouth, I tried to decide if I had a chance to get to Evan's side. I wasn't sure what I'd do once I got there, but I couldn't think of a better place to be as long as we were trapped in the club anyway.

Rick hadn't lowered his gun, which was aimed over Evan's

body and just off my left shoulder. Turning just my head, I saw O'Brian. His gun was pointed back at me.

No, not me. At Rick. What's going on?

Having Evan stuck between O'Brian and Rick, both with their guns leveled at each other, made me really uneasy. Given the choice between the two, I couldn't say which one I trusted more anymore.

I wished I had more concrete info about them both.

I wished any two other cops were inside The Firehouse instead. Or even better, the whole SWAT team.

As Evan started to slowly rise up onto his knees, their guns were aimed entirely too close to the man I loved, but I was powerless to do anything. Even if I had a gun, I wouldn't have been able to take a shot for fear that mine would make the others flinch and pull their own triggers.

Why are the two of them aiming at each other? Are there two groups of bad cops in Augusta? Is this some kind of power play move within their gang? Is anyone clean around here?

Out of the corner of my eye, I saw that one of my earlier attackers was moving. When I turned, I saw that they two still standing had flanked me.

I had no idea what to expect out of O'Brian and Rick. I couldn't take out two cops with guns, but they didn't seem to be paying me much attention anyway.

I might be able to do something about the other two thugs. My confidence quickly faded when they both pulled long knives from somewhere behind their backs. My trigger finger twitched, but my gun was locked up at the station.

All I could do was try to buy time and keep them distracted until help arrived. It was a long shot, but it was the only shot we seemed to have. I dropped into a crouch and watched for one of them to make a wrong move.

Evan's voice called out like an angel, a stupid angel that should be shutting the hell up and finding somewhere to hide.

When I glanced over my shoulder to tell him so, I saw that he'd moved. Instead of hiding, though, he'd moved to his DJ booth which would have been a great idea if it had walls rather than just being a raised platform with a wooden railing.

"James, remember how we were talking about you being my bodyguard someday?" he asked as if we were still eating ice cream by ourselves without a care in the world.

"I don't think this is the right time," I said, resuming my defensive stance and turning my attention back to the two men with the shit-eating grins who were still holding their knives aimed in my direction.

The two men were completely ignoring both O'Brian and Rick. Why not? No matter what was going on between Rick and O'Brian, all four of them were probably on the same payroll. I was just their plaything to torment while their masters worked through their own issues.

"I know you don't, baby," Evan said. "But sometimes you're too macho for your own good. Just move a little bit to your right like a good bodyguard."

Evan made no sense, but my feet moved anyway. My back was to the DJ booth and the two men were spread out a few feet apart from each other and about six feet in front of me.

"Wouldn't it be just great to be watching every movement in the crowd while I dropped the beats and the lasers danced overhead?" Evan asked.

The men in front of me looked at each other and chuckled.

At any other time, Evan's storytelling would have swept me away. It was so much fun imagining a future between us. But we had real immediate problems that I wished Evan would let me focus on.

But he didn't seem able to stop. He was just processing through his own panic, but I needed to tune it out and try to survive, for the two of us.

"I can't wait until I get those lasers," he continued. "My crappy lights are useless for anything except blinding the dancers, you know," he continued rambling.

Only he wasn't rambling, I realized. He was planning something. Something with his lights. The shitty lights off on the sides of the DJ booth that faced out toward the dance floor. With my back facing him, I wouldn't even notice the lights.

My beautiful bastard has a plan!

"The hardest part of being your bodyguard will be reminding myself to focus on the crowd instead of dancing," I said, causing confusion to spread on the faces of my attackers. Confusion was good. "I'd take a step to the left or to the right or maybe just a step backward and spin around."

"Well, we could set up times for you to dance during a break. It would all be choreographed, of course," Evan said. "You'll always lead with your left foot when I give the countdown to start the song. Like this. Three, two, one."

The stage lights flared to life. The man standing to my left got it the worst, just like Evan had hinted.

I channeled all of my pent-up rage, frustration, and fear and sprang toward him. My uppercut hit him squarely in the jaw before he even saw me moving. He dropped his knife. I wanted that knife, but knew I didn't have time. I dropped onto his chest and punched him three times in the face, hoping I'd hit him hard enough to knock him out.

When I hopped back to my feet and dropped into a defensive stance to search for the other man, he wasn't there.

The light worked against me as I searched for the other assailant.

"Don't you dare move, asshole!" Rick shouted.

Rick would be coming for me next. No matter what else happened, Rick would be the last man standing. I wouldn't stop, though. While I still drew breath, I had to just keep focusing on doing what I could.

Nearby, but somehow so far away, Evan shouted, "Help!"

I ran straight toward the DJ booth, wishing the bright lights were off so I could see what was happening.

"Whoa there, cowboy!" a man said.

Shielding my eyes from the light, I saw that the guy had his arm around Evan's neck. He'd dragged him to the far half-wall where I'd kissed Evan what felt like years ago. The man's eyes were wide open and his head was practically spinning around trying to make sure no one was sneaking up on him. A panicking criminal is one of the most dangerous. They always do such stupid shit.

I would have charged if his knife wasn't pressed against Evan's throat. He flinched every time he saw Rick and me.

How deep into the criminal organization must Rick be to instill that much fear in one of his own men, and how badly must that guy have screwed up his orders?

Or are they competing gangs?

I don't give a shit right now. I need to get Evan out of here and then we can try to piece together what is happening in this city.

Evan smiled ruefully at me. "This is some pickle we've gotten ourselves into, isn't it, James?"

I nodded, trying to look angry, intimidating and confident.

My only real option was begging, though, and I wasn't too proud to do that if it meant Evan might have a chance of getting out of there safely.

"Rick," I said, not taking my eyes off Evan. With my back turned to Rick, my shoulders tensed in expectation of him shooting me. "Just let Evan go, okay? You can do whatever the hell you want with me. Call your goon off, and let Evan walk."

"What the fuck are you talking about, you idiot?" Rick yelled back. "If you'd just shut up and tell your boyfriend to stop squirming, I might be able to do something without hurting him."

Not really processing what Rick said, I replied, "If you want to shoot Evan, you'll have to do it through me."

"I'm not trying to shoot Evan. You're dumber than I thought. Look around, dumbass."

Following Rick's order, I saw that O'Brian now had his gun pointed at me. Rick, though, had his pointed at O'Brian.

Rick was one of the good guys.

And O'Brian wasn't. My oldest friend. He'd turned bad without me even noticing. What kind of friend was I?

Well, for starters, not one who abuses his power and kills innocent people. O'Brian was almost certainly messed up in the killings. I couldn't figure out why. The answer was on the tip of my tongue, but my attention was focused on more pressing matters.

I decided that I needed to trust Rick for the next few minutes. If Rick was fucking with me, I would kill him. No amount of bullets would stop me from charging across the room and tearing his head off his fucking shoulders if he let anything happen to the one beautiful thing I had to look forward to each morning. Without Evan, what would be the point in even bothering?

"Hey, asshole!" Rick shouted. Not at me this time. His gun jerked to the right and clearly, cruelly, and unflinchingly trained on the man holding my Evan.

Be careful, Rick. Don't you dare harm a hair on Evan's head just because you think you're a superhero.

The other man jerked Evan up higher to shield as much of his body as possible.

I flinched when I heard a gunshot, but it wasn't Rick. O'Brian had taken advantage of Rick's gun finding another target. I had no idea what he'd been trying to hit, but his bullet hadn't found me.

"Stop it, O'Brian, or I'll put a bullet in your ugly forehead," Rick said.

In the middle of the chaos, my eyes locked with Evan's.

"James," Evan said, back in storytelling mode. He sounded sad, though, as if resigned to an unthinkable fate. "I think if we ever met for the first time again, I'd still fall for you. Would you be there to catch me?"

"Of course, I would," I said, hoping to keep him talking. I had a plan of my own for once. "But you wouldn't need to fall. I'd come get you wherever you were. All you'd have to do is stand there and wait for me."

"Oh yeah," Evan said.

I needed to get Evan to shut up so the other guy would focus on Rick's gun instead of me. "Rick, what are you waiting for? Take the shot. You never miss."

I knew he wouldn't shoot unless he took out O'Brian first. Even with O'Brian out of the picture, Rick wouldn't have been able to pull the trigger without a much clearer shot, but when Rick shifted his stance, it sure got the other guy's attention. He didn't even glance my direction when I started taking small, slow steps to get behind him. The DJ booth was elevated a little too high for me to get a good grip if I reached out for them.

I needed to climb up on the outside so I could grab his hand with the knife first to make sure Evan didn't get stabbed when the guy realized what I was doing. Knowing I needed to move fast, I grabbed the rail with one hand and pulled myself up onto the platform of the booth while reaching for his knife hand with the other.

The railing wiggled, making me lose my balance. Desperate to protect Evan even as I was starting to fall backward, I made one last grasp at the guy's hand and pulled it backward.

The pain was immediate. Instead of a hand, I'd grabbed the knife itself. There was no way I was letting it go, though. Not while it was still in the bastard's grasp.

Under the added weight of Evan and the man holding him, the rail gave way. Blessedly, the knife flew free as we all braced for impact.

I landed on my back with an "oof!" as the impact knocked the wind out of me.

Another shot exploded in the club. I had no idea who had pulled the trigger. Either way, that would be a problem for later.

Before I caught my breath, the attacker and Evan both landed on top of me.

With catlike quickness, the attacker spun, sending Evan rolling to the side. He started punching at my face, forcing me to protect it.

The only reprieve was when Evan hopped onto his back and pulled him off me to give me a little space to move.

It was all I needed.

I raised my knee straight into his nuts, not giving one flying fuck about whether I was fighting fair or not.

He fell off me, bent in half holding his crotch, and trying to catch his breath.

"Rick!" I shouted. "If you're still alive, handcuffs."

Rick had already closed the distance, though. He spun the perp face-down on the ground and pinned him with his knee. While reading him his Miranda rights, Rick slapped the handcuffs onto his wrists.

When Rick finished and pulled the criminal to his feet, he said, "Are you guys done needing me to save your asses?"

The only thing that stopped me from punching his smug face was knowing it would only extend my suspension, and that he was right. He had saved our asses.

The stupid prick.

"Thanks," I mumbled, pulling Evan to me to make sure he was okay.

Blood was everywhere and it was getting worse. It was on his face and shirt and—

"Knock it off, James," Evan said. "Your hand's cut and bleeding like crazy. You're getting it all over me. Let's get out of here and get you some help."

I had to actually look at my own hand to remember my injury

before I could believe that Evan really was okay. "I'll be fine," I said. "Wait. What happened to O'Brian?"

"He should be okay," Rick said. "I hit him in the shoulder. Probably passed out from the shock."

I nodded. "Fine." Turning my attention back to Evan, I said, "Fuck yeah, let's get out of here."

I threw my good arm over his shoulder and we started for the door. Together.

"That was really smart with the lights back there," I said. "I'm pretty lucky to have such a smart, sexy boyfriend."

"Are you kidding?" Evan replied. "You literally took a knife for me. I'm the lucky one."

"Take it outside," Rick growled.

Rick was still the same dick I knew and hated. But I had to acknowledge that we'd never have survived without his help. He'd never let me live it down, but it didn't matter as long as Evan was safe and we'd be able to be together.

I looked forward to questioning him and figuring out exactly what he knew and how he knew it. I had a feeling that I knew something that he might not and couldn't wait to rub it in his face.

32

JAMES

*T*he crowd cheered when they saw us emerge safely from The Firehouse. Our friends rushed forward and forced us into a group hug. The fresh air outside promised a second chance for Evan and me after it had all come so close to ending.

I certainly wasn't going to waste the opportunity.

Shrugging off our friends, I pulled Evan to me and, with all our friends and my coworkers watching, we kissed as if we were the only two men in the universe. With Evan up on his tiptoes and pressed against my chest, everything was okay with the world again.

A tap on my shoulder interrupted the moment.

Rick must have handed the handcuffed man off to another cop. He pulled me to the side and whispered, "Did you see Trey?"

"Shit. I forgot all about him. Everything was so crazy. What's his role in all of this?" I asked.

Rick glanced at my friends, but they were all too busy listening to Evan tell the story of what had happened in The Firehouse. Rick quietly said, "Trey had been working undercover.

He'd been helping us out, but a few weeks ago, something changed. I'm still not sure exactly what happened."

"He was a snitch?"

Rick nodded. "He's good at getting in where we can't go."

I shook my head, "Well, that clearly went well."

"Preaching to the choir." Rick spat on the ground. "He's a piece of shit who just happened to seem useful to some of the cops. O'Brian mostly. So no big surprise that Trey wasn't helping us as much as he was pretending, right?"

"If you have any information about, well, anything, let's talk when you get your badge back."

"Actually, I think I know something about O'Brian." When Rick raised his eyebrow, I added, "Gambling debts."

Rick shrugged. "Who doesn't toss a few bucks around on some games?"

"No, this sounded bigger. He lost big on the Super Bowl. He told me that the other day. And then probably got in deeper trying to dig his way out."

"Well, shit. It sounds like you better stop by the office tomorrow so we can pick your brain a little more rather than waiting until you get reinstated."

"So I have that to look forward to," I said with a frown.

"Whatever. You're not exactly my best bud, either."

"You hate everyone, don't you? I only hate you because you're such a pathetic dad to Jeffrey. He deserves better." My whole body had gone tense. "You stood him up the other day when it was your turn to watch him. You couldn't just suck it up and take him to the zoo like all the other weekend dads?"

Rick sighed and looked down at the ground. "Fair enough. I'm a shit dad. But I'm a good cop. So I do what I can."

"I'm sure Jeffrey will be happy to know that someday," I said, poking Rick in the chest.

He didn't even bother arguing. Instead he nodded at everyone else and said, "I've gotta go do a shit-ton of paperwork." Turning back to me, he added, "Enjoy the vacation. We'll talk when you get back."

The paramedics rolled O'Brian out on a stretcher. I wasn't sure how that made me feel. Whether he died or lived, I'd just lost one of my closest friends.

Evan must have noticed the distraction. "You okay?"

"Sure. You're okay. That's all that matters." I nodded at the ambulance. "He was more than just a cop. We were tight from day one. He was my best friend until you came along."

Evan grabbed my good hand and gave it a squeeze. "I'm sorry to hear that. I hope he's going to be fine."

"How are you doing?" I asked, changing the subject. I'd process my feelings about O'Brian some other time when I had some distance from the events.

"Scared. Shaken. Pissed." He smiled. "I'll be okay."

"We'll get you some help if you need it. Counseling or whatever. And I'll be by your side the whole way," I said giving him a hug to prove it.

"That should be enough. We'll look into the other stuff if I end up needing it."

Evan and I quickly checked each other for injuries. Other than my hand, I thought we both would just need a little rest to recover.

I flinched when he lightly touched my eye.

"That'll be black in the morning, I bet," Evan said.

"I've heard pressing meat against it helps."

Evan punched my shoulder. "Perv."

"Only for you, Evan. Only for you. Let's see what I'm going to need to do about this hand and then go home."

"Guys, one sec." The chief trotted up to us. "James, we need to talk about giving you your badge back. I want you to know I never believed the allegations, but we needed to get the facts. It looks like O'Brian was the one who took the photos and set you up. In light of tonight, I think I have all the details that I need to clear you. Can you stop by tomorrow before your shift? We can fill out the paperwork and get you back to work right away."

"That sounds great," I said, trying not to be bitter. "But if it's all the same to you, I'll stop by for a couple hours to talk, but I'm going to take the rest of the week off and spend it with my boyfriend."

The chief nodded his agreement. "That's fair enough. Looking forward to you coming back for good."

"Thanks, sir. I'm looking forward to it, too."

Turning back to the guys, I said, "I hate to run, but I don't want to spend another second down here on The Strip tonight. See you at The Firehouse soon, okay?"

I smiled when I saw Doug nodding his head, too. Watching the frenzy as the other men tried to win his attention would be entertaining for a few nights.

After another round of hugs, Evan and I checked in with the paramedics. The cut was long, but wasn't as deep as I'd feared. Once they cleaned it up and wrapped it in a bandage, we started back home.

"My place or yours?" I asked.

"Yours. Let's play cards out on your deck again and see where things go from there," he said.

I kissed the back of Evan's hand, happy to have him by my side. I'd never get tired of holding his hand.

Having him in my life, and even the light touch of his fingers, settled me.

EPILOGUE

Evan

I swallowed.

James looked down over his body at me standing at the foot of the bed and wiped the sleep from his eyes. "Damn, Evan. If you wake me up like that every day, I'll never sleep in again."

"This is waking up early? It's already ten thirty."

He groaned. "Dude, you're the one that normally sleeps in,"

"Come on. I'm just anxious and fidgety and want to get it over with. Now, get your lazy butt out of bed so we can get this day started."

"Yeah, I know. I'm getting up." James stood and stretched.

I loved that he slept naked. I loved watching those muscles flex and the tattoos dance. I loved watching his still semi-hard cock swing, threatening to hypnotize me into doing whatever he asked.

Not that I needed much convincing most days.

"Thirty minutes should give me plenty of time to shower and get dressed. We'll stop for donuts on the way out of town," James said while walking to the bathroom.

"Donuts? Again? We're going to get fat if we keep eating like that," I said.

While peeing, James said, "You'd look cute with a pooch, or are you trying to say you won't love me when I get fat?"

"When? Not even *if* anymore?"

James laughed before flushing the toilet. "Well, have you seen the older guys at the station? It's bound to happen if I stick around there long enough."

I followed James into the bathroom, not wanting to pass up a chance to have him soap up my body in the shower.

"Have you given any thought to my offer to hire you as a bodyguard?" I asked, climbing under the water after him.

"I have. But you seem to be forgetting your part of the deal."

I moaned when I felt his hand wrap around my dick and start slowly stroking me. Hiding behind the pleasure of his touch, I ignored the unanswered question and ran my hands over his chest.

James had been pressing me hard about our future, and didn't let the opportunity pass to bring it up again. "Have you even bothered to try and set up a gig yet?"

"Not yet. It's just so confusing." I didn't want to talk about it again, but I knew that James would release his grip if I tried to ignore him. My dick was so hard and his hand was already stroking me so quickly. I was at his mercy. "Getting a random gig at other little clubs around here isn't tough at all, but how is that better than steady work at The Firehouse? But coordinating any kind of a tour? I don't even know where to start. Oh, God, that feels good."

"Call that agent," he whispered in my ear. "Do it today during our drive and get it over with. You're just afraid of the uncertainty."

"And the rejection," I added.

James channeled a phrase he'd been threatening to get tattooed on me some night while I slept. "Nothing good ever comes without the risk of rejection."

"Speaking of coming," I said as I braced myself against his body and came right there in the shower.

It was crazy how easily he could make my body feel so good.

"Don't forget to bring his business card," James said as if nothing had happened. "I'm not starting the truck until you have it."

It was even crazier how perfectly well he took care of me besides just the sex. He always made sure I did the things that would make me happy, no matter how afraid I was of trying them.

"Are you sure you really want to do this today?" I asked. "We could just go back to bed and see how long until I get you off again."

"That's way too easy of a challenge. I'd rather see how long it takes you to make that call and how long we manage to stay at your family's house for this visit. Now let's get dressed and get that number dialed. The sooner you get the tour lined up, the sooner I can take a vacation and test out this bodyguarding thing."

"Fine," I said, lightly slapping his dick. "You drive a hard bargain, James, but I love you for it."

"I love you, too, Evan. You're going to blow away the world once you give them a chance to hear you. But hurry up. I need to get some donuts in me."

The End

WANT FREE BONUS CONTENT?

Sign up to the free Zach Jenkins' Fan Club to receive an exclusive free bonus scenes from future books as they become available.

Members will receive an **exclusive Fan Club only standalone novella**!

http://zpjenkins.com/newsletter-unsettled/

ALSO BY ZACH JENKINS

Firefighters on the Fox

Love on Fire

Truth on Fire

Choice on Fire

Written with E. Davies

Just a Summer Deal

Sugar Topped

ABOUT THE AUTHOR

Zach Jenkins was born in the Midwest and stayed in the Midwest until the military sent him bouncing from coast to coast and even overseas for four years. Having experienced some amazing places in this small world, he eventually settled back in the Midwest close to family and friends.

He spends most of his free time catching up with TV shows on Netflix and chasing his barking dogs away from the windows so the mailman will continue to deliver the frequent packages that Amazon keeps sending him.

IF YOU ENJOYED THIS BOOK...

Please consider leaving a review on Amazon and on Goodreads.

Find more titles by Zach Jenkins on Amazon

Want to be the first to know
about Zach Jenkins' latest release?
Want to receive his bonus stories not available anywhere else?
Sign up for his newsletter at:

http://zpjenkins.com/newsletter-unsettled/

Join me on online at:
www.zpjenkins.com

Printed in the USA
CPSIA information can be obtained
at www.ICGtesting.com
LVHW091615131023
761031LV00035B/621